**'Supposing I think we're the ~~r~~
I want to sp~~end~~**
asked.

'Then you're mi~~staken.~~
A muscle clenc~~hed.~~
children.'

'That's why I'm a paediatrician.' And why he
was one too; she'd bet her last penny.

'It's more than that, Jodie. I've seen you on
the ward, feeding babies and cuddling them—
all way beyond your job description. You even
do it when you're supposed to be off duty.'

'OK, so I love children.' She shrugged. 'So
what?'

'Jodie, you said you wanted children. One of
each, you said. But I'm infertile. I can't give
you a child. Ever.'

Kate Hardy lives on the outskirts of Norwich with her husband, two small children, two lazy spaniels—and too many books to count! She wrote her first book at age six, when her parents gave her a typewriter for her birthday. She had the first of a series of sexy romances published at age 25, and swapped a job in marketing communications for freelance health journalism when her son was born so she could spend more time with him. She's wanted to write for Mills & Boon® since she was twelve—and when she was pregnant with her daughter her husband pointed out that writing Medical Romances™ would be the perfect way to combine her interest in health issues with her love of good stories. It really is the best of both worlds—especially as she gets to meet a new gorgeous hero every time...

A BABY
OF HER OWN

BY
KATE HARDY

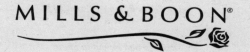

MILLS & BOON®

For Gerard, Chris and Chloë
with all my love

MILLS & BOON and MILLS & BOON with the Rose Device
are registered trademarks of the publisher.

First published in Great Britain 2002
Harlequin Mills & Boon Limited,
Eton House, 18-24 Paradise Road, Richmond, Surrey TW9 1SR

© Pamela Brooks 2002

ISBN 0 263 83105 1

Set in Times Roman 10½ on 12 pt.
03-1102-47429

Printed and bound in Spain
by Litografia Rosés, S.A., Barcelona

CHAPTER ONE

'INCEY wincey spider climbed up Amy's arch; down he came, to make our Amy laugh!'

Sam Taylor stopped dead in his tracks. He knew that voice, and it shouldn't have been singing nursery songs. He strode to the doorway of the small room—a room that was really a quarter of one of the bays in the paediatric ward, partitioned off to give more flexibility when it came to isolation nursing or a parent needing privacy— and leaned on the jamb, watching the young doctor who was playing her own version of Incey Wincey Spider with the toddler in traction in the cot, wiggling her fingers up the traction arch and then letting them drop down onto the little girl's tummy.

Her blonde curls cascaded over her shoulders, hiding her face from Sam's view, but he had no doubt she was smiling. Just like the red-headed toddler lying on the iron-framed cot in front of her, flat on her back with both legs in plaster. The ties that bound the child's legs to the traction arch were gradually moved lower and lower down the arch so her hip joints were pushed back into their proper place as her legs were stretched out.

Why was his registrar playing with a sick child when there were notes to be written up and a ward round to finish? Particularly when they were so short-staffed, thanks to the virus that had decimated the ward. Play was fine in its place, but they just didn't have time for it right now.

He cleared his throat. 'Dr Price. A word, please?'

She looked up instantly and her green eyes widened as she saw the grim expression on his face. 'Of course, Mr Taylor.' Jodie gave the consultant a brief nod, then turned back to the little girl. 'I'll see you tomorrow, Amy.' She gently touched the tip of the child's nose, the gesture telling in its affection. 'Big smile?'

'Yes, Doc-a Dodo,' the little girl lisped, doing her best to give Jodie a smile, though clearly disappointed that she was going to lose her playmate.

Satisfied that the child was happy to be left, Jodie joined Sam at the door.

'There's still half a round to do,' he pointed out tightly.

'I know.'

His steel-grey eyes narrowed. She *knew*, and she was leaving all the work to others? 'And you're playing with Amy Simcox.'

She nodded, seemingly unconcerned. 'Apart from the fact that plenty of studies show how play helps children to recover faster, it's my day off.'

Sam flushed at the double rebuke. 'I see. Well, I'm sorry, Dr Price. Though if you wore a white coat like the rest of us,' he continued, his voice very soft and very dangerous, 'maybe it would be easier to tell when you're off duty.'

It was her turn to redden now; with her fair skin, she flushed spectacularly. Literally to the roots of her hair. 'In my experience, small children are scared enough when they come into hospital. A white coat's just another barrier for the kids *and* their parents to overcome.'

'And how do the parents know you're who you say you are?' he countered silkily. 'Anyone could walk around here with a stethoscope slung round their neck and a clipboard under one arm—' just as she casually floated round the ward '—and say they're a doctor.'

'True.' She gave him an impish grin that riled him even more. 'But they don't have one of these.' She fished her hospital ID badge out of the pocket of her trousers.

He ought to remind her of her position as a junior doctor, Sam knew, but a glint in her eyes warned him she was expecting something of the sort. He couldn't be more than six or seven years older than she was, but she made him feel as if there were a whole generation between them.

'So what are you doing here on your day off?' he asked. 'Showing your dedication to the ward?' Hoping for a quick promotion, perhaps? Though that was unfair. She didn't seem the type to trample on others on her way to the top. Her dedication and enthusiasm were above question, yet Jodie Price always had time for people.

'Actually, I'm just playing with little Amy.' She bit her lip. 'Poor kid. As if it isn't bad enough being in traction at the age of eighteen months, just when she's getting used to walking, it's made worse by her father being "too busy" to visit her and her mother bursting into tears every time she sees the little one.'

'And?' he prompted, seeing the glint of tears rather than defiance in her eyes. Doctors were taught from the word go not to let themselves get so emotionally involved that it affected their judgement—but sometimes a case really tugged at your heartstrings and you forgot to be sensible.

'Her mother's convinced it's all her fault that Amy's hip joints haven't formed properly. She had three glasses of champagne on her wedding anniversary, when she was pregnant.' Jodie grimaced. 'I've told her it's not her fault, that clicky hip's fairly common in babies who were breech presentation, particularly girls. It should have been picked up even before Amy's six-week check, anyway, rather than Mrs Simcox asking her health visitor why Amy wasn't walking at sixteen months when all her peers were, then us finding out at referral that the baby had clicky hip. But she still blames herself, so little Amy doesn't get many visitors.

'I'm not saying her parents should *live* here,' she went on, lifting a hand to forestall any comment he might make. 'Parents who stay during the day need to go home at night for a proper rest—which they wouldn't get here, with monitors beeping all over the place. But I do think that a child who's stuck in one place and is old enough to talk needs a bit of company. The nurses are brilliant with her but they're overstretched.' The generous mouth thinned. 'So I've just been spending a few minutes talking to her and playing with her in my lunch-hour or before I go on duty.'

'And you do that for all your patients?'

Jodie lifted her chin, and Sam realised for the first time that she was only a couple of inches shorter than he was. Around five feet ten in the flat shoes she was wearing.

'For the ones in need, yes,' she stated defiantly.

'It can't go down very well with your boyfriend.' Why on earth had he said that?

She coloured. 'No. It didn't. Still, you have your round to finish, Mr Taylor. I won't hold you up any longer.'

It didn't. Meaning the boyfriend was history? He suddenly realised she was staring at him, expecting an answer. 'Oh. Yes. Goodnight, Dr Price.'

Sam continued on his rounds, carefully writing up his notes on each case, but he couldn't shake the image of the fair-haired junior doctor from his mind. Crazy. Even if he had been interested in another relationship—and his marriage to Angela had put him off that idea for good— it wouldn't be with Jodie. Being the subject of the hospital grapevine wasn't something he wanted to repeat. He'd been there, done that and worn the T-shirt when Angela had left him for another man.

Besides, Jodie really wasn't his type. Casual, breezy, and way too confident for a young doctor in her position. She still had a lot to learn, about life as well as medicine. *But...*

No buts, he told himself firmly. He didn't even want to be her friend, let alone anything else.

So why ask her about her boyfriend, then? a little voice in his head queried wickedly.

Slip of the tongue.

Freudian slip, more like, the voice continued. *She's beautiful, clever, fun. And you want to—*

Shut up. I've got a job to do.

He forced himself to concentrate on his rounds; then, just as he was about to leave the ward, he heard her laugh. A laugh that made him yearn, for a brief second, to have been the one who'd put a smile on her face.

'See you tonight at Mario's, Jodie,' Fiona Ferguson, the ward sister, said. 'Eight o'clock sharp.'

'I'll be on time,' Jodie promised with a grin as she sat on the edge of the desk, swinging her long legs.

'As if. You doctors are all the same, thinking that time and tide and pizza will wait for you,' Fiona teased. 'Well, if you're late, we'll just eat your share of the dough balls.'

'You wouldn't do that to a poor, starving junior doctor,' Jodie retorted, wringing her hands theatrically and laughing. 'Not where Mario's dough balls are concerned...'

'Want to bet?' Fiona threatened, laughing back.

'Still here, Dr Price?' Sam asked, sauntering up to the nurses' station.

'Oh— Mr Taylor.' Jodie's smile dimmed at the implied rebuke. 'I'm sorry. I was just…' Her voice tailed off. What was it about Sam Taylor that unsettled her so much? She'd never had a problem with her seniors before. But he was reserved to the point of being unreachable. In the six months he'd worked with them he hadn't once yet socialised with the staff on the ward. No wonder they'd nicknamed him Mr Frosty. She didn't think it was just professional distance either.

The man, she decided, needed bringing out of himself. 'Why don't you come with us tonight?' she suggested on impulse.

'With you?' He looked blank.

'To Mario's.' The way he was looking at her, she thought crossly, anyone would think she'd suggested a date, a candlelit supper for two. 'There's a crowd of us going. It's a regular thing. On Thursday nights, they have a jazz band playing—not heavy stuff, more your Nick Drake jazz-folk sort of thing—and they do the best pizza in the city. The risotto's good, if you don't like pizza.' So he couldn't use that as an excuse.

'I—'

'Eight o'clock. And we don't talk shop *all* night.'

Excuse number two neatly sidestepped, he noticed with sudden amusement.

'And partners are welcome.'

Circumventing excuse number three? Or was she fishing to see if he was involved with someone? No. Of course she wasn't interested in him. She'd made it clear it was a group event which happened every week. 'I—'

'Good,' she said, before he could think up a valid reason to refuse. 'See you there, then.' She gave him directions to the restaurant. 'It's the little Italian place with a green sign outside—just ask for the hospital table when you get there. They'll know who you mean. Bye, Fi,' she called to the sister. And then she was gone in a swirl of soft hair, brightly coloured tunic top and black trousers, leaving Sam staring after her and Fiona with raised eyebrows.

When Jodie had changed into an elderly pair of leggings and swapped her loafers for a pair of trainers, she fastened her hair back into a ponytail, shrugged on her waterproof jacket and headed for the bicycle sheds in the far corner of the hospital car park.

What *had* she done? Jodie asked herself as she unlocked her bike, slid her handbag and document case into the waterproof carrier on the rear wheel and started cycling home. Fancy inviting the ward's newest consultant to their crowd's usual Thursday night gathering! He'd think she was trying to curry favour. Or, worse, that she was trying to net herself a husband with a prestigious job and a good income.

And she didn't fancy Sam Taylor. Not at all.

Though he was attractive enough, if you liked the strong, silent type. Tall, dark and intense. Grey eyes that reminded her of a rainy Wednesday morning, lonely and forgotten. She preferred the athletic type. Blond and suntanned, rather than that fine, pale skin. Curly, unruly hair, not straight and brushed back neatly from his face. Someone who wasn't too serious, saw the sunny side of life. With a mouth that smiled a lot and crinkles round the eyes—and she liked cornflower blue eyes.

Oh, stop thinking about it! she told herself, skidding to a halt outside her house. He probably wouldn't even turn up.

CHAPTER TWO

However, when Jodie arrived at the small Italian restaurant at a quarter past eight—'just in time for the last garlic dough ball,' as Fiona commented with a grin—Sam Taylor was sitting at one end of the long table. Opposite the only spare chair, she realised with dismay. Wearing plain black trousers and a matching cotton round-neck sweater—trust him to do the Man in Black routine.

And it looked even better on him than she would have guessed.

Ignoring the rapid pounding of her heart, she sat down and gave him her most professional smile. 'Hi. So you made it.'

He nodded.

Not going to make it easy for me, are you? she thought crossly. 'Has everyone ordered?'

'Yes, and we ordered for you,' Mick Salmond, one of the few male nurses from the paediatric ward, told her. 'Your usual. Margherita with mushrooms, black olives, Dolcelatte and avocado.'

'Cheers. You're a mate.' She wrinkled her nose at him.

'Avocado? On *pizza*?' Sam lifted one eyebrow.

For the first time, Jodie saw amusement in his eyes. And suddenly that rainy Wednesday morning was gone: in its place was a sultry silver. And although his mouth wasn't smiling widely—just a tiny lift at one corner—it had lost that vulnerable look. Instead, it looked… kissable.

Her mouth went dry. No. Absolutely not. No way was she going to start thinking of Sam Taylor in those terms.

Drop-dead gorgeous or lame duck? That was what her brother would have asked if she'd told him she'd been stupid enough to invite the consultant on their Thursday night pizza run—reasoning that either Sam was drop-dead gorgeous and someone had dared Jodie to do it, or he was another of Jodie's lame ducks. Earlier today, she'd have said lame duck. Now she wasn't so sure.

To cover her confusion, she nodded to the jazz band, a trio of singer-pianist, double-bass player and drummer, who were setting up for the night's session. 'They're very good.'

'So I've been told.'

She grabbed a bottle of red wine from the table and poured herself a glass, then took a large sip. 'Mmm, that's better,' she said in satisfaction.

'It's the one you discovered last month,' Fiona told her. 'The Sicilian job.'

'Trust a woman to find a wine that tastes of chocolate,' Mick said, rolling his eyes. 'It was on the "Specials" board. "Red wine with a chocolate finish." And *she* was in charge of ordering, that night, so we didn't get any choice.'

'Come on. You know you like it. Anyway, red wine and chocolate are good for you. You've read the studies in the *Lancet*.' Jodie grinned broadly.

General hooting greeted her words.

'And then there's that study on pleasure. People who enjoy themselves have better immune systems. It's all to do with SIgA.'

'Enough of the lectures, Jo-jo.' Mick ruffled her hair. 'And, please, don't anyone mention the P-word.'

'The P-word?' Sam asked, mystified.

'P-l-a-y.' Mick spelled it out in phonics, amusing Jodie even more. 'She's writing some article or other for the *British Medical Journal* about the importance of play in paediatrics, how it helps children get better.'

'So that's why you spend all your free time on the ward, playing with certain patients?' Sam asked.

She flushed. 'Yes. No. I just enjoy my work, that's all.'

The pizzas arrived, diverting everyone's attention. Jodie had eaten three mouthfuls before she realised that Sam was staring at her. 'What?' she asked.

'I can't believe you're actually eating that.' He made a face.

'Don't knock it until you've tried it.' Jodie cut another piece, making sure there was a slice of avocado on it, and speared it with her fork. 'Here,' she said, reaching over towards him.

Again, there was that silvery glint in his eyes and he bent his head to taste the pizza, his gaze locking with hers. Jodie's mouth went dry again. She hadn't eaten since a snatched half a sandwich for lunch, so the wine must have gone to her head. What *was* she doing, feeding him from her fork? And what must he think of her?

Embarrassed, she almost snatched her hand back.

'Better than I expected,' he said.

She could feel her face burning. Was he referring just to the pizza, or to her, or to the evening? And, come to think of it, why was he here? True, she'd pretty much steamrollered him into it on the ward—but he could have just not turned up and made an excuse the next morning.

Jodie decided to take refuge in her pizza. Maybe when she had some good, solid carbohydrates inside her, she might start thinking more clearly.

'What made you decide on paediatrics?' Sam asked, startling her into looking up at him.

'I like children,' she said simply.

'But you're not married, not planning any of your own?'

Jodie's eyes narrowed. Why was he asking? So he could decide not to recommend her for promotion, since she didn't have any real commitment to her job—she was going to give up work to have kids and waste all her years of training?

No, of course not. He wasn't one of the old school, the sort who couldn't help discriminating against young female doctors. He treated everyone on the ward alike—polite and distant. He was just trying to make conversation. It wasn't his fault he'd touched on her sore point. Three months ago, her ex-boyfriend Graham had told her she spent too much time on her career and he wanted to start a family almost as soon as they were married. Not that he'd actually asked her; he'd just assumed she'd fall in with his plans. When he'd realised she wasn't prepared to give up her job, he'd walked out on her.

'No, I'm not married, and I'm not planning a houseful of kids,' she said tightly, still seething inwardly at the memory of Graham's parting shot that she'd be a lousy wife anyway—she couldn't even cook! 'Not all women want children, you know.'

'Don't they?' asked Sam, his face completely unreadable.

'No. I'm an honorary auntie—well, godmother to my best friend Ellen's little boy, Billy—and that suits me fine.' Actually, that was a bit of a fib. She did want children, just not yet. Not until she'd figured out how to raise a family without throwing away all those years of studying and working silly hours. And then there was the small matter of finding a suitable father...

That rainy Wednesday morning look was back in his eyes again. Children were obviously a sore point with him, too, Jodie thought. Not that it was any of her business.

Time to change the subject. 'Why did you decide on paediatrics?' she asked.

'I...' He wasn't going to tell her the whole truth. 'I did a stint in Paediatrics after I qualified. I went to Cardiology after that, then Oncology—but I found that I liked working with children best.' Even though it was like rubbing salt in the wound.

'Cardiology.' She looked thoughtful. 'I nearly did that, too. Because of Sadie.'

'Sadie?'

'My younger sister.' Her green eyes were suddenly sombre. 'She had a hole in the heart. There wasn't anything they could do at the time. She died when she was two weeks old.'

'Was she much younger than you?' he asked gently.

Jodie shook her head. 'I was nearly three at the time. My brother, Matt, was seven, so he remembers more about it than I do. Anyway, when I decided to become a doctor, he was the one who said I should give myself time to find out what I was really interested in, not rush straight into heart surgery or neonatal so I could save future Sadies. We had a huge row over it, but I have to admit he was right.' She smiled wryly. 'He rang me tonight, actually. He's getting engaged—at last. He and Annie have known each other since junior school but they only realised their feelings for each other a month or so back. Now they've decided they've wasted too much time already, so the engagement party's this week-end.'

'And you're on duty?' Sam guessed.

She nodded.

He tipped his head on one side. 'Can't you swap shifts with one of the others?'

'Not when we're almost skeleton staff.' She shrugged. 'Ah, well. Matt and Annie'll come up for the weekend some time soon and we'll have a party of our own. Just the three of us.'

So the boyfriend was *definitely* off the scene, Sam thought. Though he wasn't sure if she was upset about it or not. Jodie had seemed touchy when he'd mentioned children—maybe the boyfriend hadn't wanted them and she had.

But he couldn't get involved with her. One, she was a colleague; two, she was probably on the rebound; and, three, maybe she'd sort out her differences with her ex and they'd get back together.

But he couldn't take his eyes off her. Even when they were both talking to other people, and she'd shifted places to drink her coffee at the other end of the table and chat to Fiona Ferguson, he was aware of her. Aware of every move she made—the way her blonde curls cascaded over her shoulders, the way her bright purple silk shirt highlighted the intense green of her eyes. Aware of the curve of her mouth. His body tightened and he suddenly wondered what it would be like to kiss her. To tangle his fingers in that silky soft hair, to feel her mouth soften and open under his own, her hands against his bare skin…

He took a deep breath. Hell. What was it about Jodie Price that got under his skin? He'd always been so scrupulous about keeping work and his private life separate.

Not that he had a private life. Just himself and the cat who'd adopted him when he'd moved to Norfolk. Not the children he'd once expected to have by this age. Not a little boy climbing everything in sight and wanting to help Daddy make a tree-house and listen to his heart with Daddy's stethoscope and go to the park together to sail a model yacht on the boating lake. Not a baby girl just starting to walk, tottering on unsteady legs towards her father with a beaming face and chubby outstretched hands when he walked in the door, greeting him with a loud 'Da-*da*,' and a stream of delighted babbling.

He locked his hands together under the table, squeezing his fingers hard until the physical pain took his mind off his mental torture. Half the conversation tonight had been about children—particular cases on the ward who'd touched everyone's heart—or handing round the latest family snaps to be admired. It was why he always avoided social events at work, so he didn't have to smile and smile and pretend the yawning gap in his own life didn't exist. The yawning gap that even dedicating himself one hundred per cent to his job didn't fill.

He caught himself watching Jodie again. The way she laughed, throwing her head back, her whole face lighting up. The way she looked earnestly at whoever she was talking to, making them feel as if they were the only person in the room. The way her eyes crinkled at the corners...

Oh, get a life, Taylor, he told himself wryly. Nothing's going to come of it. Ever.

When everyone had finished their coffee and gradually drifted home in twos and threes, sharing lifts and taxis, Sam and Jodie were left in the doorway of the restaurant.

'How are you getting home?' he asked.

'Pushbike.'

He frowned. 'In this rain?'

She shrugged. 'It's only about three miles between here and my place. Fifteen minutes, tops, if I catch all the traffic lights on green.'

'But you'll get soaked.'

'It won't kill me. You can't catch a cold from getting wet, Doctor,' she reminded him, wrapping a scarf round her glorious hair.

'Where's your bike?'

'I...er... Why?'

'Because you're going to stop being stubborn, put your bike in the back of my car and let me give you a lift home. It's the least I can do,' he said, making her close her mouth on the argument she'd been about to produce. 'You were kind enough to ask me to join you tonight.'

You plural, not you singular, she reminded herself. 'I...er...' Oh, why was she suddenly so inarticulate?

'Where's your bike?' he asked again.

'Chained to that lamppost,' she said, pointing to the elderly and slightly battered racer she'd inherited from Matt fifteen years before, on her thirteenth birthday, and had liked too much to replace with a newer—or more feminine—model.

'Keys?' he asked, holding out his hand.

She shook her head, unlocked the bike herself, and wheeled it alongside him to his car. 'Are you sure about this?' she asked, eyeing the four-wheel-drive doubtfully. It was big enough to cope with her bike, but it was also pristine. And, judging by the number plate, less than six months old.

'Sure.' He opened the back and hauled her bike inside. 'Hop in.'

Being in an enclosed space with Sam Taylor was a

definite mistake, she thought. It was a big car, but she was still very much aware of how close he was to her. If she shifted her hand less than six inches, her fingers would brush against his. Fingers that were gentle with his patients. How would they be with her?

Stop it, Jodie, she told herself fiercely. And yet she couldn't help remembering the look in his eyes as she'd fed him pizza. She could imagine them lying in the park on a sunny day, with his head in her lap as she fed him seedless grapes and morsels of Brie—and then bending down to kiss the crumbs away from his lips...

That's the last time you ever drink more than one glass of wine in his company, Jodie Price, she warned herself.

Then she flushed as she became aware that he'd been talking to her, and she hadn't heard a single word he'd said. 'Sorry. I was miles away,' she apologised.

'Where do I go from here?' he asked.

He sounded completely cool and calm. Obviously he didn't feel the same pull and she'd be wise to remember that. Dragging her thoughts together, she directed him through the back streets of the city to her small terraced house. He parked the car and hefted her bike down.

'Thanks for the lift.'

'No problem.'

Should she ask him in for coffee? It was only polite, seeing as he'd given her a lift home, but she didn't want him misreading her motives.

In the end Sam made the decision for her. 'Goodnight, Jodie.'

It was the first time he'd ever used her name, and she wasn't prepared for the sudden lurch of her heart. 'Goodnight,' she muttered, not quite daring to use his first name but not wanting to rebuff him by using a more formal mode of address.

She watched him as he drove away. She still knew virtually nothing about him, despite having spent most of the evening talking to him. He was as mysterious and distant as ever. Though there had been a moment when she'd thought she'd come close to breaking through his wall.

Shaking her head, she walked into the house. Maybe he didn't want to be rescued. But that sultry silver in his eyes told her that she couldn't give up. Not yet.

As he drove away, Sam could have kicked himself. Why had he insisted on taking her home? He'd been so close to breaking a personal rule. When he'd taken her bike out of the car, the way she'd looked up at him, her eyes all shiny and her mouth so soft and warm and inviting… His body had been screaming out for him to take her in his arms and kiss her, and to hell with the consequences.

But the sensible side of him had overruled it. Just. Apart from the fact that affairs with colleagues were bad news, he'd sworn he'd never get involved again. Not after his extremely messy divorce.

Come off it. What have you got to lose? Angela's the complete opposite of Jodie, the voice in his head taunted. *Just look at her.*

Angela was petite, slender and well groomed, and she only ever wore little suits teamed with designer shoes, handbag and briefcase, whereas Jodie was tall, curvy and had a much more casual attitude towards clothes. Angela's make-up was always immaculate, whereas Jodie's barely existed—he suspected that the nearest Jodie came to cosmetics was a lip-salve. Angela would never have dreamed of letting her expensive haircut get wet—and if she'd had a bike it would have been an expensive and trendy mountain bike, not a battered, elderly racer.

Maybe that was the attraction: Jodie was the opposite of Angela. No, that was unfair. Jodie was a little like the Angela he'd fallen in love with at university, the young lawyer with a sparkle in her eye and a sense of fun that had stopped him being too serious.

The sparkle that had soon dimmed when Angela had discovered what a failure Sam had been as a husband—that he couldn't give her what she most wanted in the world. And it would be exactly the same with Jodie. It might start out fine, full of love and laughter, but over the months it would change and one day he'd come home to an empty house and an apologetic note. Just like he had with Angela.

Though what was he doing, even thinking about Jodie in those terms? She wasn't interested in him and he didn't have the right to get involved with anyone. Not with his past.

She said being an honorary auntie was enough for her, the little voice reminded him.

Only because her biological clock hasn't started ticking yet.

She was serious. She's dedicated to her career.

Now, maybe. Things change. She's a natural mother. You can see it in her eyes, in the way she acts with the children on the ward.

But supposing—

Supposing nothing. It's *not* going to happen.

CHAPTER THREE

'I'M JODIE PRICE,' she said, extending a hand to the pale-faced woman who was sitting holding a small baby. 'And this is Dr Taylor, who's sharing the assessment clinic with me.' Mr, actually, but she'd learned that it was easier to say 'Doctor' than go through all the explanations about when you got high enough up the career ladder, you swapped Dr for plain Mr or Ms. Worried parents weren't interested in the social niceties: they just wanted reassurance about their sick children. Right now.

She glanced down at her notes. 'This is Harry, yes?'

The woman nodded.

'And he's seven weeks old.'

Tears welled in the woman's eyes. 'He's so small… I thought it was just a cold. And then he couldn't breathe…'

'You're here now and we can help him, Mrs Bartlett,' Jodie soothed, crouching down beside her and focusing on the baby. 'Let's have a look at the little fellow and see what's going on. Can you tell me a bit about his symptoms? When did you first notice he was ill?'

'Two days ago. He picked up his sister's cold—but he wouldn't feed properly yesterday, only took half what he normally has, and he started coughing. Then, today, he was so quiet…I thought I was probably fussing too much but I took him to the doctor anyway—and she sent me straight here.'

'To the paediatric assessment unit. I know, it sounds scary, but you're in the best place,' Jodie reassured her.

'All it means is that we're specialists in babies and children, so we'll be able to work out what's wrong with him and how to treat him quicker than your GP can. Now, let's get this vest and nappy off.' She quickly undressed the baby, weighed him and measured his length, and noted the details on his chart. 'He's a lovely big boy, isn't he?'

'Yes. My husband's tall.' Mrs Bartlett gulped. 'He's parking the car. Laura's with him.'

'Laura's Harry's sister?' Jodie guessed.

'Yes. She's three and a half.'

'The perfect age gap. My brother's nearly four years older than me,' Jodie said. 'Young Harry here's going to hero-worship her from the minute he can toddle. I was just the same with Matt.' She put a thermometer under the baby's armpit, and waited until it bleeped, then looked carefully at the reading. 'That's good, he doesn't have a high temperature. Apyrexic,' she said to Sam, who was writing down what she said.

The baby coughed, and gave a hoarse cry.

'Lost his voice, has he?' she asked sympathetically.

Mrs Bartlett nodded. 'He's a happy baby anyway, doesn't normally cry a lot, but now he can't even tell me when he's hungry or wet.'

Jodie replaced the baby's nappy, noting the way the skin underneath the baby's ribs and the base of his throat sucked in sharply every time he breathed. Pretty much a textbook case. 'Tracheal tug,' she said to Sam. She turned to Mrs Bartlett. 'I'm going to listen to his chest now.' She placed her stethoscope on Harry's chest. 'Hmm, he sounds pretty wheezy. Creps,' she said to Sam. 'There are a few bubbles there, Mrs Bartlett—that means there's lots of mucus clogging up the tubes.' Gently, she palpated the baby's abdomen. 'His abdomen's fine.' She took her otoscope, the instrument used for checking the ear canal, and looked in the baby's ears. 'Bilateral wax,' she said to Sam, then turned back to Mrs Bartlett. 'He's got a fair bit of wax in both ears—he's really bunged up with that lurgy, poor love.'

'It's just a cold, then?' Mrs Bartlett looked hopeful.

'It's a little more than that, I'm afraid. There's a rather nasty virus going round called RSV or respiratory syncytial virus. I'll need to take a sample of his nasal secretions to check if that's what he has—all I'll do is put a tube up his nose so we can suck out some of the mucus and send it off to the lab for them to run a few tests. It looks a bit scary but it won't hurt him,' she reassured Mrs Bartlett. 'And then I'll put a probe on his foot so I can make some more checks. The light goes through his foot and hits the probe—again, it won't hurt him, because it's just like having a very soft strap wrapped round his foot—and that helps me measure the oxygen levels in his blood, his pulse rate and his breathing.' She indicated the machine next to the bed. 'It'll probably bleep a lot, but don't worry—these things don't take into account the fact that babies tend to wriggle! The minute they move, the alarm goes off—it'll probably say something like ''insufficient light'' on the screen, and all that means is that he's moved so the probe needs to be reset.'

Quickly, Jodie took the sample of the nasal secretions, then wrapped the cuff of the probe round Harry's foot. As she'd suspected, his oxygen saturation was a little on the low side and his pulse was rapid. 'Sats eighty-seven in air, pulse a hundred and sixty.' She watched the child's chest rise and fall, keeping one eye on the second hand of the clock as she counted his breaths in her head. 'Resp sixty-five.' She brushed her fingers momentarily against the baby's face. 'You're having a tough time, little one, but hang on in there. We'll sort you out. We're going to admit him for a few days, Mrs Bartlett,' she said. 'All the signs are that he's got bronchiolitis, which is usually caused by RSV. In adults and older children, it just gives you a bad cold and a cough, but in young babies it tends to make them quite poorly.'

'He'll be all right, though?' Mrs Bartlett's eyes were wide with anxiety.

Jodie nodded. 'It's very common—there's often an epidemic between November and March. We've got six babies on the ward with it already, so he'll be in good company.' She gently rubbed Harry's cheek again. 'You did the right thing in bringing him in to us. He hasn't got it that badly, though I should warn you that they often get worse before they get better. He'll be in for somewhere between three and seven days, depending on how he responds to treatment, and he'll be coughing for a good six to ten weeks after he gets home, maybe even until the clocks go forward.'

'So you can do something for him?'

Jodie nodded. 'The problem is that some of his airways are so small—less than a tenth of a millimetre across—so the mucus is gumming him up and making him wheezy. We'll try giving him a nebuliser—that's just a mask with a drug in it—to help widen his airways a bit, and he'll breathe the drug in through a mist of oxygen. That might help him to feed a bit better. We may need to give him some oxygen, too. We'll do it through a tube under his nose, which looks frightening but won't hurt him. And if he's finding it too tiring to feed—bearing in mind he's having a hard time getting his breath, he's only got the energy to take a bit of his usual feeds at the moment—we'll feed him through an nasogastric tube.

What that means is a tube goes up his nose and into his stomach, so he'll get all the goodness he needs without having to work so hard for it.'

Mrs Bartlett looked shocked. 'Can we—can I stay with him?'

'Of course you can. He'll be in a room on his own because the virus is highly infectious and we don't want it spreading to the other children. There'll be a notice on his door saying that he's in isolation nursing, but all that means is that the nurses and doctors will wear a gown and gloves when they come into his room to stop the virus lingering on their clothes or their hands and then spreading to other patients on the ward. This particular virus can live for around twenty minutes outside the body, on clothes, which is why it spreads so quickly.'

'I see.'

'There's a chair-bed in the room, and you'll be able to use the staff restaurant when the public restaurant's closed,' Jodie added. 'And we have a policy of shared care in the ward, so you'll know at all times exactly what's going on, what you can do to help and what we need to do.'

Mrs Bartlett still looked stunned at the idea of her child being hospitalised.

'There's a visitor phone on the ward. Parents and visitors answer it, rather than the ward staff, and that means you can take any incoming calls without worrying that you're stopping important calls coming into the ward. There's a payphone just outside the assessment unit, too, though I'm afraid we have to bar mobile phones because they could interfere with the equipment,' Jodie warned.

Mrs Bartlett nodded.

'Give Harry a cuddle while I finish writing his admission notes,' Jodie said, 'and I'll ask Alice, the dark-haired nurse over there, to take you through to the ward. If your husband and Laura haven't arrived by the time you go, I'll make sure someone brings them through to you.'

'Thank you, Dr Price.'

'That's what I'm here for. Alice will give you an information sheet about bronchiolitis and RSV, which should answer most of your questions.' She smiled. 'I'm on duty later tonight, so I'll see you when I do my round and we can have a chat then if you have any other questions or you're worried about anything.'

When Mrs Bartlett had left, cradling the baby in her arms, Sam turned to Jodie. 'You're good with parents. You explained everything to her without being patronising. Well done.'

'Thank you.' She was surprised at the compliment. He'd barely spoken to her since he'd dropped her home from Mario's the previous week, so she'd been dreading it when she'd realised that he was going to be with her on the paediatric assessment unit shift this morning. She'd expected him to pick up every single fault, however minor. Instead, he'd let her get on with it and had only occasionally offered an opinion, phrasing it more as a question so she could show off her own knowledge of the subject.

'You're a good doctor, Jodie,' he said, surprising her even further. 'Though are you sure about the nebuliser?'

'I know it's controversial and some doctors don't approve of using bronchodilators,' Jodie said, 'but if it helps the baby breathe, that's the most important thing. We'll trial Atrovent and salbutamol, see which one works best for him. Sometimes they respond to one better than the other.'

Sam grinned. 'Yes, Dr Price.'

She flushed. 'Sorry. You already knew that.' Of course

he did. He was a consultant, with a good six years' more experience than her. Trust her to open her mouth and say something so stupid, just when she was trying to prove to him that she could be a cool, calm and rational colleague.

Not to mention proving to herself that Sam Taylor didn't make her hormones run amok.

'I'd always rather you explain yourself than make assumptions,' Sam said gently, as if sensing her embarrassment. 'It leaves less room for errors.'

'Right.'

'What else have we got in?' he asked.

'An asthma attack—when I know the history, I might suggest some skin tests to see if the girl's allergic to cats or dust mites or any particular sorts of food, and I want to check whether the parents smoke round her—plus two rashes and a possible fracture.'

'Lead on, Macduff,' he misquoted with a grin.

Jodie stared at him for a moment, slightly dazed. That grin could only be described as dazzling. What was it about the man? Since Mario's, he'd as good as avoided her. And just when she'd decided that he was remote, glacial and not worth thinking about, he did or said something that made her look again, see him as a man—a very attractive man, at that. Without that wall of reserve, he'd be devastating.

It couldn't work out between them. There were too many barriers, social *and* professional, so why couldn't she stop that voice in her head telling her to go for it?

Not now. They had work to do. 'Let's go,' she said, forcing herself to smile at Sam in her best professional manner.

The voice grew louder over the next week until it was positively deafening. The departmental Christmas party was traditionally held in the middle of December; those who were married came with their partners, but those who were single—which meant most of their ward, as the staff were all fairly young—picked the name of their partner out of a hat, the day before the party.

And Jodie had picked Sam. Completely by accident, but it felt as if fate or some higher power had done it by design. She'd agonised over it for nearly the whole of her shift. Should she give him the option of backing out, or use the chance to break down his reserve? He'd hate it. Hadn't he gone back into his shell since Mario's? On the other hand, it was the Christmas party—and Christmas was a season of magic, when everything could change.

When Sam had finished his ward round, she caught his attention. 'Mr Taylor—could I have a word, please?'

'Of course, Dr Price.'

The formality made her nervous, but she pressed on. 'Um...your office?' she suggested.

'My office,' he agreed.

Sam's office was the same size as that of Lyn Trevor, the other paediatric consultant, but whereas Lynn's desk sported pictures of her husband and children and the walls were decorated with pictures drawn by patients and her own children, Sam's office was completely devoid of personal touches. Not even so much as a pot-plant graced the window-sill and even the Christmas cards were stacked in a neat pile on his desk rather than being on display.

Jodie felt even more daunted. Everything around her screamed, *Keep off! Don't touch!*

He sat down on the swivel chair behind his desk. 'So, what can I do for you, Dr Price?'

She took a deep breath, gathered up her courage and swallowed hard. 'It's about the departmental Christmas party, tomorrow night,' she muttered.

'Yes?'

'I…er…I picked your name out of the hat. It means I'm supposed to go with you.'

Not a flicker of emotion. He was completely unreadable—and unreachable. 'And?'

'I…' she floundered. 'Look, if you'd rather I made some excuse and didn't go…'

'Why would I do that?'

'Honestly, men could be so *dense* sometimes!'

To her shock, he laughed.

'What?'

'I take it you didn't mean to say that out loud?'

Jodie clapped a hand over her mouth, horrified. 'Oh, no. Please, tell me I didn't…' When he said nothing, she closed her eyes. 'I'm sorry. What I meant was—'

'Given that the first half of the party is a revue, and Mr Frosty's bound to have a part in it, you think I'd find it too embarrassing to attend,' he finished.

Her eyes widened. He knew about his nickname on the ward?

He folded his arms. 'Yes, Jodie, I know.'

'I'd see a specialist but there isn't a cure for foot-in-mouth disease,' she said wryly.

'You didn't say a thing this time. You have one of those faces that shows every single thought.' Still, his own expression was unreadable. 'Do I take it you'd rather not go to the party with me, then?'

'I…' She sighed. 'I don't know.'

'Explain.'

'Do you always have to be so, so…' Unable to find

the word she was searching for, she growled in frustration.

That at least raised a smile. 'Difficult?'

'Something like that.' Well, he'd asked. If he didn't like the answer, that was his problem; she couldn't keep quiet any more. 'When you came to Mario's with us, I thought you'd, well, thawed out a bit. And then...'

'Back to Mr Frosty.'

'Yes.' This time, Jodie had the grace to blush. 'I guess Fiona didn't ask you before she put your name in the hat.'

'No.'

'If you'd rather not go, I won't make a big deal out of it.'

'And if I do go?'

'Um, there's the revue.' Jodie winced. She didn't know a huge amount of detail, but what she knew wasn't good.

'Consultants are fair game for sketches. And I suppose it's time the boot was on the other foot.'

Jodie digested his words and then blinked hard. 'You mean—you've acted in a revue?'

He shrugged. 'I think all doctors get involved in some kind of revue at some point. When I was a house officer, I played our senior consultant as God.'

'No.' Without thinking, Jodie perched on the edge of his desk and crossed one long leg over the other. 'Show me.'

'Show you?'

'Oh, come on. You can't feed me a line like that and back off again.'

He shook his head. 'I can't really remember the lines now. It was something about the ten commandments of working on his ward. Thou shalt not drink coffee until thou hast knelt at my feet and worshipped me for five minutes—that sort of thing.'

'Hmm.' Jodie's smile was pure mischief.

'Don't even think about it,' Sam warned, guessing at what was going through her mind. 'Are you in this revue?'

She shook her head. 'I'm a hopeless actor. I just made some of the props—with a bit of help from some of the older children on the ward.'

'Such as Mr Frosty's costume?' he asked.

'I think it's time I left.' She gave him a nervous smile, slid down from his desk and headed for the door.

'Not so fast.'

She stopped with her fingers on the doorhandle.

'Am I picking you up or meeting you here? And what time?'

'I'll make my own way there,' Jodie said. 'It starts at seven in the canteen.'

'I'll see you there, then. At ten to seven.'

'OK.' Jodie left his office, closing the door behind her, and heaved a sigh of relief. It hadn't been as bad as she'd expected…or, now she thought about it, had it? She had her date for the party, but she still had no idea whether he really wanted to be there or not.

'Well, Mr Frosty, if the revue doesn't thaw you out, nothing will,' she said softly to herself.

Sam leaned back in his chair. He was walking on very thin ice indeed. Jodie had even given him the perfect get-out for not going to the party—so why hadn't he jumped at it?

Because you want to see her all dressed up, the little voice in his head informed him. *And then you want to take every scrap of material off her again…*

Do not.

You're in denial—Mr Frosty, the voice taunted him.

Sam groaned aloud. He was going to have an awful lot to live up to—but he was aware that distance wasn't a style the ward was comfortable with. Maybe the party was his chance to show the rest of the team that he had a sense of humour, that he could laugh with them.

How long had it been since he'd laughed? Really laughed? Before Jodie had burst into his life and insisted on him going to Mario's with the rest of the team?

He closed his eyes. Jodie again. Maybe he should have accepted her get-out. He wasn't sure how he was going to cope, dancing with her. Holding her so close and knowing he couldn't have her—ever. It wouldn't be fair on either of them.

He smiled wryly. Who said life had to be fair? Besides, he knew there were people out there far worse off than he was—it was just that, right now, it didn't feel like it.

Tomorrow morning, he decided, he'd have a convenient sore throat. One that got worse during the day so he wouldn't feel up to going to the Christmas party. That way, Jodie wouldn't think he was avoiding the party because of her. She'd still be able to go and enjoy herself, she wouldn't be embarrassed dealing with him at work—and he wouldn't have the torture of wanting something he knew he couldn't have.

CHAPTER FOUR

THOUGH, of course, Sam did nothing of the kind.

Although his path didn't cross Jodie's during their shifts the next day, he could have complained about his 'sore throat' to any of the nurses or junior doctors he worked with, knowing they'd pass the message on to Jodie. But something stopped him and at ten to seven he was striding down the corridor to meet her.

She looked absolutely stunning, Sam thought as he saw her standing by the entrance to the canteen. She'd piled her hair on the top of her head and little tendrils escaped here and there to soften the severity of the style. Her make-up was understated, just enough to emphasise her beautiful green eyes and tempting mouth. And the crimson raw silk shift dress suited her colouring perfectly. Not to mention showing just how long her legs were. She was wearing heels high enough to make her the same height as he was and a smile that made him feel as if a knife had been plunged into his stomach—because the smile was directed at the man who was talking to her. Mick Salmond, a nurse on their ward. The man who knew her well enough to order her pizza for her when she'd been late at Mario's.

And the warmth of that smile... Was something going on between them? He searched his memory. Wasn't Mick Salmond married? What the hell did Jodie think she was doing, having an affair with a married man?

'Dr Price,' he said stiffly, joining them. 'I trust I'm not late.'

35

'No. I was early.'

'For once,' Mick said, teasing her.

'Huh. I'm not late all the time.'

'Only on a day with a Y in it,' the nurse retorted with a grin.

'Yeah, yeah. Hey, Mick's got some fabulous news.' She dug her companion in the ribs. 'Go on, *tell* him, before I burst.'

'News?' Sam echoed, frowning.

Mick beamed. 'I'm going to be a dad!'

'Congratulations.' Sam forced the word out. Hadn't he come to terms with this years ago? So why could those six little words still hurt him so much, the six words he'd never be able to say himself?

And why was Jodie going to burst? Was *she* the one expecting Mick's baby?

The thought was like a physical blow. He felt winded, sick.

'Shelley's going to make a brilliant mum,' Jodie said. 'And she's asked me to be godmother.'

Shelley? Godmother? The fog cleared and Sam suddenly realised what was going on. Jodie wasn't having a baby. She was just excited for her friends and delighted at being asked to be godmother. So when it came to her own babies, she'd—

'When it's your turn,' Mick said to Jodie with a grin, echoing Sam's tortured thoughts, 'I bet you'll never get any housework or anything done. You'll spend the whole day playing with your kids.' He gave her a sidelong look. 'Observing them at the same time. And you'll write it up as a study paper when they're in bed.'

Jodie rolled her eyes. 'I will not. I'm not that bad, Mick.'

'Yes, you are, Jo-jo. Look at the way you are with the

kids on the ward. You even come in on your days off to play with some of them. You'll be ten times worse with your own,' he teased.

'No, I won't. I'll be just like any other mum.'

'As if!' he scoffed. 'I can see you with half a dozen.'

Jodie chuckled. 'Yeah, right.'

'So how many are you planning?'

She shrugged. 'Depends.' Her face softened. 'One of each would be nice.'

'You mean, so you get to play with the trains *and* the doll's house?' he teased.

'Let's p-l-a-y,' Jodie teased back.

Just like any other mum. The words reverberated inside Sam's head, numbing his senses. *Just like any other mum.* Meaning that Jodie, despite her protests at Mario's, was planning to have children one day. *One of each would be nice.* Taking it for granted that she could have children—and so could her future husband.

'Can't you just see what our Jodie'll be like with her kids, Mr Taylor?' Mick asked, laughing.

'Yes,' Sam said shortly. He could just see Jodie with her arm round a three-year-old, reading him a story and getting him to act out one of the speaking parts while the baby was curled up asleep on her lap. *I'll huff, and I'll puff, and I'll blow your house down…* He could imagine only too clearly the softness in her face, the deep enduring love of a mother in her eyes as she cuddled her children.

A stab of something—pain or envy—lanced through him as he listened to them talking about their future children. It amazed him how easily they could talk about their plans. If anyone had asked him, the words would have stuck in his throat. *I can't have babies. I'm infertile.*

He became aware that Mick was talking again. 'I

dunno who called it morning sickness. Shelley gets it in the evenings.' As if he'd sensed the message behind the sharp look Sam had given him, Mick continued, 'I would have stayed with her to hold her hand and mop her face and what have you, but she wanted me to video the revue so she doesn't miss out on it.'

'Indeed,' Sam said brusquely.

'Mick wr—' Jodie stopped abruptly, suddenly realising she'd been about to blurt out that Mick had written the revue. 'Shall we go and sit down, Mr Taylor?' She didn't quite dare use his first name. Not when he was back in Mr Frosty mode. And why the sudden freeze? Something was obviously bugging Sam…but what?

I'll be just like any other mum… One of each would be nice…

The words echoed round and round in Sam's head as if his mind were stuck on continuous-loop replay, and he couldn't stop it, even though it was torture. And the dreams he'd started entertaining about Jodie crumbled into dust.

He sat locked in misery until he realised that Jodie was shuffling in her seat, looking distinctly nervous. Then he realised why: the revue. It had been going on for ten minutes and he hadn't even noticed.

He forced his attention to the stage. Yes, there was Mr Frosty: a consultant in a formal suit, a white coat and a snowman's head, with an expressionless mouth, large grey eyes and a big carrot for a nose.

Stuart Henderson, one of the senior house officers, was playing Mr Frosty and had Sam's mannerisms down to a T. Sam found himself laughing at the way various nurses pretended to be overcome with heat and Mr Frosty cooled them down by blasting snow at them. Jodie visibly relaxed when she saw Sam laugh. He found himself relaxing, too. Maybe he was reading too much into all this, overreacting. Hadn't Angela always said he was too serious?

Finally there was the pièce de résistance—something Jodie obviously hadn't expected, by her gasp of surprise followed by a giggle—the pantomime dog. One of the auxiliaries had made herself up like an English springer spaniel and trotted onto the stage, dropping a ball on the patient's bed and saying, 'Let's play!' She bounded up to every other actor on the stage—'doctor' and 'patient'—saying, 'Let's play! It's good for you. Let's play!'

'Hoist with your own petard?' Sam whispered in her ear.

'Deservedly.' Though she didn't look cross or embarrassed by the lampooning—just amused. In her shoes, Angela would have stormed off in a huff.

When the revue finished, Sam gave some of the loudest applause. He also collared Mick when they'd both helped to shift the chairs out of the way of the dancing area.

'I…er…hope you weren't offended,' Mick said, shuffling his feet slightly.

'If it weren't for your impending fatherhood,' Sam said coolly, 'I'd be suggesting that you consider a change in career.'

Mick looked completely crestfallen, and Jodie—who'd joined them and had overheard Sam's comment—was clearly about to jump to his defence when Sam added, 'Your comic timing's brilliant and you've an eye for detail and mannerisms. But nursing's a steadier job than scriptwriting, so I'd stick with the day job for now. Besides, we'd all miss you too much on the ward if you went off to London.'

Mick stared at the consultant, open-mouthed. 'For a minute there, I thought you were going to...' He tailed off awkwardly.

'Freeze you?' Sam gave a rueful smile. 'Message received and understood.'

'Thanks for being such a good sport about it,' Mick said.

'Hmm. Well, another lesson's been drummed into me tonight.' With a sidelong glance at Jodie, he explained, 'Play's good for you.'

Jodie's face clashed spectacularly with her dress. 'I'm not really that over the top, am I, Mick?'

The other nurse nodded. 'But the patients love it.' He looked diffidently at Sam. 'And they think a lot of you, too, sir.'

'The name's Sam, not sir,' Sam corrected.

'Sam.' Mick smiled. 'Well, have a good time, you two. I'm off to get some banana and anchovy pizza before I dare go home and show the missus this.' He waved the video camera at them and headed for the exit.

'Banana and anchovy?' Sam and Jodie simultaneously pulled faces.

'Am I really like a spaniel?' Jodie asked Sam.

He tipped his head on one side, considering. 'Well, I don't see any evidence of a wet, shiny nose, big brown eyes, long ears or halitosis.'

Her colour deepened. 'That isn't what I meant.'

He smiled. 'Your enthusiasm keeps everyone going.'

'Oh.' Jodie bit her lip. 'Shall we get something to eat?'

'As long as it isn't banana and anchovy pizza.'

'Definitely not!' They wandered over to the buffet table and helped themselves to chicken satay, tiny bridge rolls and cheese straws. Jodie eschewed the mince pies in favour of chocolate cheesecake, and ate Sam's share as well as her own.

'I had you pegged as a traditionalist,' Sam said.

Jodie grimaced. 'I hate mince pies. And Christmas cake. And Christmas pud.' She screwed up her nose. 'I don't care if dried fruit's good for you, it's revolting.'

Sam's lips twitched. 'So you have chocolate instead?'

Jodie spread her hands. 'Chocolate's actually quite healthy.'

'That report about catechins was referring to top-quality plain chocolate,' Sam said, surprising her. 'And it didn't say you should eat industrial-sized quantities of the stuff.'

'You weren't eating your cheesecake,' she pointed out, 'and it'd be a shame to waste it.'

'Huh.' Sam gave a mock grimace and the corners of his eyes crinkled.

Jodie felt her pulse accelerate and looked away. Not now. No, please, she couldn't develop a huge crush on the man *now*. She was supposed to be getting him out of his shell, that was all. Though a part of her wanted to do much, much, more…

As the band started, Sam looked round and raised an eyebrow. 'Is that Stuart Henderson again, on vocals?'

'And air guitar. A man of many talents,' Jodie said. 'Not to mention a string of nurses desperate for his attention.' She shrugged. 'He's young.'

Sam burst out laughing. 'You're starting to sound like me.'

'You mean, old?' she teased.

'Listen, you, I'd hardly started at infant school when you were born.'

'Uh-huh.' Jodie tapped her nose meaningfully. 'I believe you.'

To his surprise, Sam was thoroughly enjoying himself. How long had it been since he'd had some fun? Excluding Mario's...too long, he thought. When his marriage had disintegrated, he'd buried himself in work and avoided the social side of hospital life completely.

Right now, he wanted to have fun. And if Jodie thought he was an old fogey, she was about to learn something! 'Come on. Let's dance,' he said to her.

'Dance?'

'Move your feet, wiggle about a bit in time to music, that sort of thing.'

Was this really Sam Taylor, Mr Frosty, talking? Jodie thought. But the offer was too good to resist. 'Let's go,' she said, putting her plate down on a convenient table.

Dance. She'd expected him maybe to do what everyone else at the party was doing—as he'd put it, 'move your feet, wiggle about a bit'. But, no, Sam Taylor could *really* dance. When Stuart's band switched to a rock 'n' roll number, Sam was spinning Jodie round and getting her to do all sorts of complicated things that would have had Matt goggling at his clumsy kid sister's performance.

When the music stopped, she was out of breath. And then she became aware that she and Sam were the only two on the floor—everyone else was standing watching them, applauding and cheering. Yet again that evening Jodie's face clashed with her dress, and she retreated to the table where she'd left her plate.

'Come on. Play's good for you,' Sam teased.

'Not this sort of play. I've got two left feet.'

'I didn't notice.'

'You were leading me.' She paused. 'I didn't know you could dance like that.'

'I'm a bit out of practice.'

'Could have fooled me.' If that was out of practice,

heaven only knew what he'd be like when he was back in the swing of things!

'Oh, Mr Taylor…' a breathy voice asserted beside them.

Melissa the Maneater from the neonatal unit, Jodie thought with a sigh, recognising the brunette in the skimpy dress.

'I was very impressed with your…' big pause '…dancing. Could we?'

'I believe I'm Dr Price's partner for this evening,' Sam said, stepping closer to Jodie.

'Jodie won't mind, will you, sweetie?'

It was more of a command than a question. Jodie lifted her hands in surrender. She had to face it: men preferred small and slinky, not strapping and Amazon. In any contest with Melissa, she'd lose. 'Be my guest.'

It was another fast number, and Sam dutifully twirled Melissa round the floor and somehow managed to evade her clutches for the next dance. Jodie merely sat on the sidelines, watching him and wondering what made him tick. One minute he was Mr Frosty, completely unreadable; the next he was shy and retiring; and now here he was, the star of the dance floor. She couldn't work him out.

Four dances later, he was back at her side. 'You're supposed to be my partner for this evening.'

'So?'

'So, dance with me. Come on, Doc-a Dodo. Playtime.'

So he'd heard Amy's pronunciation of her name, a nickname that half the ward staff had adopted. She flushed deeply. 'I—'

'Dance with me, Jodie.' The sultry silver gleam in his eyes made her nod mutely and join him on the dance floor.

She wished she hadn't when the music suddenly turned soft and Stuart started to sing a ballad. Sam drew her closer so that she was forced to put her arms round his neck for balance, and they swayed together in time to the music. She could smell his clean, fresh scent so clearly; the feel of his arms round her, together with the sweet seductive spell of the music, had her resting her head on his shoulder a few moments later.

Sam rested his cheek against her hair. He'd thought this would be a test he couldn't cope with, holding Jodie in his arms. But it was easy. So very, very easy. She felt right; she belonged there. Her skin smelled of honey, and she was warm and soft and sweet and…

He couldn't help himself. Her neck looked graceful and her skin was soft, and he couldn't resist touching his lips to the curve of her neck. And once he'd kissed her there, he couldn't stop. She felt so good. He needed to touch her, taste her. He trailed his lips up towards her ear, soft butterfly kisses, and felt her tremble in his arms.

So she was affected by this as much as he was.

'Jodie,' he breathed softly in her ear.

'Yes?' She lifted her head to look straight into his eyes. Hers were very green and very large, and her mouth was too tempting to resist.

His lips were just millimetres away from hers when the music changed again, to a bouncy, uptempo song. They'd both been in so deep that they hadn't even heard the ballad finish and Stuart introduce the next number. Shocked, they pulled apart and stared at each other. They'd almost kissed—in front of just about all their colleagues.

'Mr Taylor?'

'I, er, yes, Megan.' Sam forced himself to smile at the young nurse who'd interrupted them.

'Could I have this dance, please?'

He looked at Jodie, who spread her hands. 'It's a party. You're meant to dance.'

'Then let's dance, Megan,' Sam said.

Relieved at being let off so easily, Jodie made a quick exit to the loos. She was still shaking from that almost-kiss, and she nearly tripped several times because her knees were still doing jelly impersonations. How could she have been so stupid? Not only had she joined in with the lengthy skit in the Christmas revue, targeting Sam's remoteness, she'd almost let him kiss her in front of everyone—meaning that everyone on the ward would tease them mercilessly for weeks!

What would that kiss have been like? When he'd taken her into his arms, every single nerve-end had been aware of him. She'd felt the lean hardness of his body against hers, been aware of the strength in those arms and yet also the gentleness. Her temperature had risen sharply and the lightest touch of his lips against her skin had sent desire shooting through her. She'd felt her breasts swelling, her body softening with need for him. And if his mouth had found hers...

She leaned against the washbasin, staring at herself in the mirror. Her eyes were over-bright and her lips were red and swollen, as if he'd actually kissed her. And kissed her very thoroughly indeed. 'You look a complete state, Price,' she told her reflection. 'And what *did* you think you were doing?' Though she didn't particularly want to hear the answer to that.

'Are you all right, Jo-jo?' Fiona asked, coming in to find Jodie in a dream.

'Just tired,' Jodie lied.

'Well, that'll teach you to burn the candles at both

ends. Doctors nowadays—no stamina,' Fiona teased. 'By the way, just what did you do to Mr Frosty?'

'Nothing!'

Too swift, too hot a denial, Jodie realised with horror. She'd just made things ten times worse. Thank God Fiona wasn't one of the gossip-mongers, or she'd really have been in trouble.

'Well, whatever you said to him, he's been human to-night. More than just the clever doctor who terrifies the hell out of the staff. If you can keep him out of his shell, Jo-jo, I think we'll all benefit,' Fiona said thoughtfully.

'It isn't up to me.'

Fiona's lips twitched. 'Let's play!'

Jodie laughed. 'I'll never live that down, will I?'

'Not for a while,' the ward sister admitted, smiling.

Finally, Jodie pulled herself together and returned to the dance floor.

'At last.' Sam materialised beside her almost instantly. 'You OK?'

'Just tired,' Jodie said. 'I think I'll call it a night.'

He nodded. 'I'll drive you home.'

She shook her head, mindful of Fiona's comment. Nobody wanted Sam to go back into his shell, but on the other hand she didn't think she could spend much more time in his company without making a complete fool of herself. 'Stay and enjoy yourself,' she said. 'I'll make my own way back.'

'You will not,' said Sam. 'For a start, there's no way you could have cycled in wearing that dress.'

'Taxi,' Jodie informed him. 'I'm just going to call one.'

He shook his head. 'I'm not waiting out in the cold with you when my car's just round the corner.'

'You don't have to wait.'

'Yes, I do. You're my partner for this evening,' he reminded her. 'So stop arguing. I'll drive you home.'

How could she resist? 'Yes, sir,' she said meekly.

He didn't say much on the way out to the car park, and no one commented that they were leaving early—they were all too busy enjoying themselves. Jodie climbed into Sam's car and he drove her home. She noted that he didn't need to ask directions. Clearly he'd remembered the way to her house from Mario's.

When they arrived at Jodie's house, she looked at him. 'Would you like to come in for a coffee?'

His face was unreadable. 'Thanks, but I really ought to be going.'

'Of course.' Jodie hoped that her disappointment didn't show on her face. He was right, anyway. If he came in for coffee and the fire between them started again, and he kissed her, and— She caught her thoughts. No. Not now. Not now, or she'd end up throwing herself at him and embarrassing them both. 'Thanks for the lift,' she said quietly.

'Pleasure.' He paused. 'Jodie…'

Every nerve was suddenly aware of him. Was he going to kiss her? She looked at him, wide-eyed, and her tongue came out to moisten her dry lips.

He was going to kiss her. She could see it in his eyes. Even in the shadowy depths of the car, she could see the sultry silver gleam—he wanted her as much as she wanted him. Now he was going to reach up, cup her face and slowly lower his mouth to hers. He was going to nibble at her lower lip until she opened her mouth and kissed him properly, and then—

'See you on Monday,' he said.

'Right.' She banked down the intense surge of disappointment. How stupid could she get? Of *course* he hadn't been about to kiss her. That almost-kiss, before, had been in the heat of the moment. They'd been in the middle of a party, with soft music playing and everyone around them full of Christmas cheer—they'd both been carried away by events around them, that was all. He wasn't going to kiss her in the middle of the street in his car on a freezing cold night.

Or anywhere else, for that matter, or he'd have taken up her offer of coffee.

'See you,' she said, trying to sound as neutral as possible. She climbed out of the car and closed the door very carefully—although she felt more like slamming it, she didn't want Sam to think her a sulky, childish brat.

Sam waited in the car, watching until she'd unlocked her door and was safely inside. Then he closed his eyes and rested his head on the steering-wheel. He'd been so close to losing his head. He'd wanted to drag Jodie into his arms and kiss her senseless. He could still remember the feel of her skin against his mouth and it had taken all his will-power to refuse her offer of coffee. If he'd accepted, he knew he'd have spent the rest of the night in her bed, their bodies tangled together even in sleep.

Even the thought of it made his body ache unbearably. There was still time to change his mind. All he had to do was walk down the short path to her front door. Say he'd love a coffee, if the offer was still open. And then hold her again, hold her and kiss that soft, warm, inviting mouth…

But what then? He had a nasty feeling that one night with Jodie wouldn't be enough. He didn't have the right to ask her for more—and she deserved more. A lot more. From someone who'd be able to offer something better than a short affair or long-term misery. He couldn't offer her a future—not the future she wanted, anyway. She wanted a normal life with a normal husband. Which meant not with him. And there was no point in starting something he couldn't finish.

From now on, he was going to stay out of her way.

Thus resolved, he straightened up, started the engine and headed for home.

CHAPTER FIVE

SAM was definitely avoiding her, Jodie thought. Maybe she'd scared him off—maybe he'd thought 'coffee' had been a euphemism for sex and that was why he'd refused.

Her skin heated. She'd actually meant just coffee—but, yes, she'd wanted him to kiss her as well. And if she was honest with herself, she'd wanted more than that. Much more.

She still did.

She growled at herself. She really had to stop day-dreaming about him. Yet, now she knew what it was like to be held in her arms, she wanted it to happen again. And again.

Three days later, after discussing the problem with her best friend Ellen and a large box of chocolates, Jodie decided to leave it until after Christmas to tackle Sam. She'd be working over the holidays, so she wouldn't have time to start brooding about him, and then she was off to stay with her family. When she came back from Yorkshire, she'd see how the land lay.

In the meantime, she concentrated on her job. Amy Simcox was back in for her check-up, and this time Jodie was relieved to see that Amy's mum had pulled herself together.

'Doc-a Dodo!' Amy greeted her with a beam. 'Mummy, look, is Doc-a Dodo!'

'Hello, Amy.' Jodie ruffled the little girl's hair and sat down on the edge of the bed. 'So how are things going?' she asked Mrs Simcox.

'The surgeon says she's going to be fine—the X-rays show the operation was a success, so he isn't going to have to put her in traction again.'

'That's good.'

'And she can have the plaster off for Christmas.' Mrs Simcox blinked away tears. 'It's the best Christmas present I could have asked for. Thank you so much.'

'Hey, I didn't do much.'

'You spent a lot of your time with her, talking to her. That nice Sister Ferguson told me all about it.'

'It's my job,' Jodie said. 'And Amy's a lovely little girl.'

'Thank you. From the bottom of my heart.'

'Any time. That's what we're here for,' Jodie assured her. 'And I expect you want to be getting home, so I'll say goodbye now. Bye-bye, Amy.'

'Bye-bye, Doc-a Dodo.'

Jodie grinned. 'Everyone calls me that now, you know! Take care.' She squeezed Mrs Simcox's shoulder. 'Everything's going to be fine.'

The next patient on her list was another bronchiolitis victim. Poppy Richardson was the eighth on the ward right now, and she wouldn't be the last. Little Harry Bartlett had recovered well, but Jodie still hated the virus and the deep hacking cough that left the babies exhausted and the parents worried sick.

She put on the gown that hung on the back of the isolation-room door, added a mask and gloves and checked the obs chart. Fourteen-week-old Poppy had been in for three days and was getting worse. The previous night, the nurse had had to put in a nasogastric tube and increase the level of oxygen the baby was being given. Poppy had tried to pull the tubes out, small as she was, so they'd needed to use surgical tape to keep them in place.

Poppy lay in the metal-framed cot, a towel rolled into a horseshoe shape at her feet, to stop her slipping down under her sheet, and a similar one around her head. There was a musical mobile hanging above her—one of the hospital's stock, judging by the non-matching dangling toys and the way the musical box was tied on with ribbon—and either her parents or one of the nurses had tried to make the room more festive by twining bright red tinsel on the metal bars at the head of the cot.

'Poor little love. You're having a tough time, here,' Jodie soothed as she removed the sheet. The little girl's face was red and one of the nurses had stripped her down to her vest to keep her more comfortable in the heat. Yet again, Jodie was annoyed by the way the heating system at the hospital was so inflexible. It was always either too hot or too cold, and it was almost impossible to adjust.

Jodie examined the little body as quickly as she could, then filled in the charts and wrote her plan in the notes. Continue oxygen to keep the sats up; consider a trial reduction tomorrow if the sats stayed above 90; trial of normal feed but use NG if needed to give the baby a rest; check respiration between 30 and 50. Just as she finished writing, the monitor began bleeping. With a sigh, Jodie tucked the folder of notes back in the pocket on the door, refastened the probe and pressed the reset button on the monitor.

'Thanks, Jo-jo,' Mick said, coming into the room. 'These monitors…'

'Yeah.' Jodie replaced the sheet. 'Poor little mite. It's tough on the parents, too, at this time of year.'

'The Richardsons live twenty miles away, and they've

got three-year-old twins. They visit as much as they can, but…' Mick shrugged.

'It's going to be a rough Christmas for all of them. Are you on?'

Mick shook his head. 'I'm doing New Year. You?'

'Yep. Well, I'm single—it's not as important for me to have Christmas Day off as it is for someone with a family.' She gave a dismissive wave of her hand. 'It's only another day.'

'Jodie Price, what *are* you like?' Mick teased. 'Listen to her. "Only another day." It's Christmas, woman.'

'And we'll pull the stops out as usual to make it as good as we can for the patients. I take it Richard's doing his usual stint as the Red-Coated One?'

'Yes, and then it's the buffet for the staff and parents in the evening. Madge is making her sausage rolls.'

Madge was the ward orderly and always reminded Jodie of an old-fashioned housekeeper, plump with grey curly hair, rosy cheeks and a twinkle in her eye. According to all the staff on Paeds, she made the best pastry in the world. She always brought in mince pies and sausage rolls at Christmas, and a plate of old-fashioned lemon-curd tarts when it was a staff member's birthday.

'Yum. Not to mention all the boxes of chocolates from grateful parents,' Jodie said with a smile.

'Which will all be gone by New Year, because the doctors round here are all chocoholics. Or shall we say that one of them in particular is? I bet your pockets are stuffed with wrappers already!'

Jodie cuffed him lightly round the ear. 'Enough of your cheek, Salmond.'

He grinned and did a begging-dog impersonation. 'Let's play!'

'Oh, you!' Jodie couldn't help smiling as she removed

the gown, mask and gloves and moved to the next bay. Two more bronchiolitis patients—there was a definite epidemic this year so it was no wonder that a lot of the staff had also caught the virus, coming down with sore throats and bad colds. At least these two little ones were on the mend and might be allowed home on Christmas morning. Dutifully, she wrote up her notes and walked to the next bay.

Ellie Langton was asleep. Jodie smiled at the eight-year-old and resisted the temptation—just—to smooth back her glossy dark curls. Ellie had been diagnosed with Graves's disease—also known as hyperthyroidism or thyrotoxicosis—two years before. The autoimmune condition meant that antibodies in her blood reacted to stimulate her thyroid gland, which meant in turn that the chemical processes in most of her cells were accelerated. Jodie glanced quickly through the notes. Ellie's had been a classic case—she'd started to become anxious and had had disturbed sleep and nightmares, her schoolwork and handwriting had both deteriorated, she'd had a rapid pulse even when asleep, plus an increased appetite combined with weight loss. She hadn't had the protruding eyes sometimes associated with the condition and her thyroid hadn't been obviously enlarged—the GP had originally suspected a psychological disturbance—but a blood test had shown elevated levels of thyroxine in her blood.

When Ellie had been diagnosed, she'd been given drug treatment to reduce the secretion of thyroxine. She'd tolerated the drug well, but she hadn't been one of the lucky twenty-five per cent who recovered spontaneously within the first two years of drug treatment. As soon as the drugs had been stopped, her condition had recurred, so she'd been given radioiodine. The downside of the treatment was that it destroyed the thyroid gland, so Ellie would have a lifetime of taking drugs to counteract hypothyroidism.

Currently, she was still under observation but there was a more than fair chance that she'd be home for Christmas.

Jodie glanced over the record of Ellie's observations. Yes, she'd definitely be home for Christmas. A miracle, in her parents' eyes: they'd have their daughter home again and well.

Ellie was the last patient and Jodie mooched over to the nurses' station.

'All done?' Mick asked.

She nodded.

'Want to talk about it?'

She shrugged. 'Nothing to talk about.'

'Hmm.' Mick looked as if he didn't believe her, but he didn't press the point. 'Go on, home with you. We'll see you tomorrow.'

'Yeah.' Jodie found it hard to summon up her usual enthusiasm. Maybe the cycle ride home would help. Once the endorphins were flowing, it would help her shake off this sudden dullness...she hoped.

It didn't. And when Christmas Day dawned, Jodie had to admit why she felt so miserable.

Sam.

She hadn't seen him since...it felt like for ever. She assumed that he was away over Christmas, though she hadn't actually checked the duty roster. Christmas on their ward usually meant Lyn would work half-days and be on call for emergencies, so they were covered for senior staff. She and the other junior doctors would do the bulk of the duty.

Sam could have sent her a card, she thought crossly, but he probably hadn't sent anyone on the ward a card. Mr Frosty clearly didn't believe in Christmas. The Christmas party had been an aberration. She was beginning to wonder if she'd dreamed the whole thing.

She did the ward round as usual with Megan and Sheila, wishing various parents as happy a Christmas as possible and delighting others by signing release forms so the children could go home for Christmas. The tinsel-festooned reindeer horns she wore were a hit with all the children, as were the small gifts she gave them wrapped up as crackers—socks for the babies and little tubes that mooed or baaed or chirped when you turned them upside down for the older ones. Particularly when Jodie herself gave a half-decent impersonation of 'Mooey Christmas' or 'Merry Chirpmas' to go with them.

She'd just finished writing up a set of notes when she heard, 'Ho, ho, ho!'

Father Christmas—but the deep voice wasn't that of Richard, the head of Paediatrics. She peeped round the corner of the bay and did a double-take when she recognised the figure in the red costume, white beard and hair.

Since when had Sam been on duty? His name wasn't on the whiteboard near the nurses' station—or had she missed it, subconsciously blocking it out?

'Ho, ho, ho. Merry Christmas, everyone!' He spent a few moments with each child, talking to them and giving them special gifts from Santa. Money collected by the Friends of the Hospital group had paid for each child to have an appropriate gift—a sleepsuit for the babies, colouring books and crayons for the toddlers and a book or jigsaw for the older ones—and every little face had lit up as Father Christmas had swept in. There were gifts for siblings who'd been dragged away from the presents under the tree at home, too, selection boxes of sweets and gift vouchers donated by the local department store. The hospital mascot—a huge bear called Willoughby— would be along later with a bucket of fun-sized chocolate bars, and someone had brought in a CD player with Christmas songs and carols to give more of a party atmosphere.

'Merry Christmas, Sister,' Father Christmas said to Fiona Ferguson at the other end of the ward, and to Jodie's surprise he whipped a sprig of mistletoe from his sack and held it over her.

Mr Frosty, under the mistletoe? Giving Christmas kisses?

No way. She had to be dreaming.

She continued on her rounds, checking observation charts, writing down her findings and reassuring worried parents.

'Merry Christmas, Megan. Merry Christmas, Sheila.' Both were subjected to the mistletoe treatment, and both giggled and kissed him on the cheek.

Just when Jodie thought she'd escaped his notice, he boomed, 'Merry Christmas, Dr Price!'

'Merry Christmas, Santa,' she replied gravely.

He waved the mistletoe at her. 'Come on. Just for Santa.'

His eyes were unreadable, and her knees suddenly turned to water. She couldn't possibly kiss him in the middle of the ward... But if she didn't, it would make her feelings for him even more obvious. Why couldn't he have just left her alone?

'I—I'm in the middle of my rounds.'

'Ho, ho, ho. I'm in the middle of my rounds, too!' Santa informed her.

Sam had avoided her for over a week and now he expected her to kiss him. The nerve of the man! She thought about kicking his shins—but too many people were watching and she was aware of the ever-vigilant hospital grapevine. She didn't want to make matters even worse.

He waved the mistletoe at her again. 'Merry Christmas.'

She gave in and moved to kiss his cheek—except he moved at the same time, turning his face so that she kissed his mouth.

What happened next, she couldn't say for sure, but the next thing she knew one of the older children was whistling loudly and several of the parents were clapping. Jodie's face matched Santa's coat, and Santa's eyes were most definitely silver.

'Happy Christmas,' he said in a strained voice.

'Happy Christmas,' she croaked back, and fled to her patient in the next bay.

CHAPTER SIX

SAM watched Jodie go with dismay. He hadn't intended that to happen. He'd thought maybe a kiss from Father Christmas would break the tension between them and let them return to some sort of friendship...but it hadn't. If anything, it had made the situation a whole lot worse.

Because the minute that his lips had touched hers, he'd been lost. The friendly peck on the lips he'd intended had turned into something much, much hotter. Thank goodness he was wearing the Father Christmas suit and no one could see the effect she'd had on him.

He sighed inwardly. He'd apologise to her later—once he'd worked out what he was going to say. If he went after her now, he'd only end up kissing her again. How could he resist, now he knew what she tasted like? Now he knew how her lips fitted his so perfectly? 'Ho, ho, ho. Merry Christmas, everyone,' he said, and continued with his round, smiling and producing presents from his sack.

'Shouldn't you be having a cold shower instead?' Fiona Ferguson asked, nodding at the mug of tea Jodie was holding.

'Very funny.' Jodie glowered over the edge of the mug.

'Well, you've certainly thawed our Mr Frosty,' Fiona said dryly. 'Who'd have thought he'd take over from Richard as Father Christmas? Much less with mistletoe!'

'He kissed you, too,' Jodie pointed out. 'And Megan. And Sheila.'

'Jodie, sweetheart, hasn't anyone told you there's a difference between a peck and a kiss? We got a peck—and you got one hell of a kiss.'

'It didn't mean anything,' Jodie muttered.

'Didn't it?'

Jodie sighed. 'Not to him.'

'Oh, dear.' Fiona opened a tin of chocolate-covered Viennese biscuits and offered it to Jodie. 'Take several. It sounds as if you need them.'

'I...' Jodie munched on a biscuit. 'I don't know what's going on. First we're friends, then he freezes me out again. He changes like the weather and I don't have a clue what's going on in his head. And now today, he—Oh!' She growled in frustration.

'He's probably as confused as you are, pet.'

'Pet?' Jodie snorted. 'I'm only eighteen months younger than you, Fi.'

'Figure of speech. Jo-jo, why don't you just talk to him?'

'When?'

Fiona shrugged. 'When you've summoned up your courage. Bleep him.'

'And what do I say?'

She raised an eyebrow. 'This isn't like you. You're normally so sure of yourself.'

Jodie made a face. 'Professionally, yes. This is different.'

'You always fight for what you believe in—so why back off now?'

'Because,' Jodie said, 'I don't know what I want—or what he wants.'

'Put it this way,' Fiona told her, 'you were the only one to get a slow dance out of him at the Christmas party.'

'By accident.'

'He spoke to Stuart Henderson before he came to dance with you.'

Jodie blinked. 'You mean, he...?' No. Surely not. Surely he hadn't asked Stuart to play something smoochy so they could dance together cheek to cheek?

Fiona shrugged. 'I don't know. Ask Stuart.'

'And start the hospital grapevine? Sam wouldn't appreciate that.'

'I wouldn't dream of gossiping,' Fiona said, looking askance at the rebuke. 'And you know it.'

'Of course I do—but not everyone's like you.' Jodie took another sip of tea. 'I dunno, Fi. It's all going to go wrong.'

'How do you know until you give it a try?'

'I just do. Can we change the subject?' Jodie ate another biscuit.

'Sure. But you'd be good for each other,' Fiona said, ignoring Jodie's pained look. 'And I still think you should give it a try.'

'I'd better get on with some work,' Jodie said. She drained her tea. 'Thanks for the biscuits.'

'Any time. And you know where I am if you want to talk. Confidentially,' Fiona added.

'Thanks, Fi. I appreciate it. Really.' But right now she didn't want to talk or even think about Sam Taylor.

Jodie decided to avoid Sam completely and slip quietly out of the ward when she'd finished her shift, rather than staying on to have a Christmas drink with the night staff. By dint of rushing to the loo or discussing a patient with the parents whenever she saw him heading in her direction, she managed to avoid him for the rest of the morning and she didn't go for a lunch-break until she was sure that he was back from his and she wouldn't bump into him in the canteen. She just about managed to force down the turkey-and-trimmings lunch, passing on the Christmas pud in favour of a piece of fruit, and she had no idea what she talked about to the others on her table because, despite her determination, she couldn't get Sam and that kiss out of her mind.

He was in the paediatric assessment unit all afternoon, to her relief, as it meant she didn't have to see him at all. Though she should have known that it was going too well, because fate stepped in. Literally. The minute that she finished her last observation and report, she opened one of the double doors to leave the ward and walked straight into him.

'Are you OK?'

She shot backwards as if she'd been burned. 'I'm fine,' she mumbled.

'Jodie, I've nearly finished in the PAU. You were on early as well. I'll give you a lift home.'

She shook her head. 'I've got my bike.'

He sighed. 'It's sleeting out there.' He lifted a hand to forestall her protest. 'Yes, Jodie, I know you're perfectly capable of cycling home, but why freeze when you can stow your bike in my car and be home at the same time as if you'd done it the hard way but still be warm and dry?'

'I…' There was no answer to that. And she had a nasty feeling that he'd make her explain exactly why she didn't want to be anywhere near him if she protested. 'Thanks.'

'I've just got to sort out some paperwork. I'll see you in…' he glanced at his watch '…a quarter of an hour?'

She nodded.

It was more like half an hour, but she hadn't minded waiting. She'd caught up with some of the journals she'd been meaning to read since finishing her paper on the role of play in recovery periods. Plus Fiona had given her a huge handful of chocolates, and she'd steadily munched her way through them to dispel her nervousness.

'Sorry I'm late.'

'No problem.'

'Ready?'

She nodded and put the journals into her bag. 'So how was your afternoon?' she asked.

'Typical PAU at Christmas. Little kids pretending to be grown-ups and taking a big swig of brandy or whatever, then being ill afterwards—worse still, some of the older generation actually give them the stuff in the first place!' He rolled his eyes. 'Honestly. "It was only a little sip, Doctor. I didn't think it would hurt. Not when it's Christmas." They didn't realise that a child has a much lower body weight so one gulp for them is equivalent to a full drink for an adult. And then they get stroppy and start huffing about how it never hurt their own children or themselves, so they don't see why I'm making such a fuss over it.'

'Ouch.'

'Yeah. Well, they won't do it again. Not when they've been forced to witness the resultant stomach pump to get all the toxins out of the child and save it from alcoholic poisoning. And then we have toys with small bits being scattered all over the floor and the baby swallows one or the toddler stuffs it in an ear or up a nostril.' He groaned. 'I hate Christmas.'

She'd already gathered that.

He gave her a sidelong look. 'Sorry. It's just cases like that make me so angry. Children are so precious. Why can't people take more *care* with them?'

'Because there's so much going on at Christmas that half the time they're caught by surprise,' Jodie said quietly as they reached the bicycle sheds.

'I suppose you're right. It still gets to me, though.'

Children. What *was* it about Sam and children? He'd given off all the signs that he didn't want any of his own—and yet any man who reacted like that to the usual Christmas crises really cared about children.

She didn't dare ask him, though: it was too much of a risk, and she didn't want him being Mr Frosty with her again. She unlocked her bike and wheeled it slowly alongside them as she followed him to his car. He hefted it into the back, and she climbed into the passenger seat.

Sam drove to her house in silence, and Jodie wasn't sure how to break it. Finally, he pulled up in her road. 'I'll get your bike out for you.'

'Thanks.'

He vaulted from the car and hauled her bike out from the boot. 'Here you go.'

'Thanks for the lift.'

'Pleasure. And it wasn't out of my way, before you say it.'

They were both aware that they hadn't discussed the subject that had been in both their minds for most of the day, yet neither of them wanted to be the one to broach it.

'I...er... Would you like to come in for a coffee or something?' Jodie said.

'Yes,' Sam's mouth said, ignoring the polite refusal that his brain had intended to make.

Was that yes to coffee? Jodie wondered. Or to something?

He locked the car while she wheeled her bike to the

front door. She unlocked it, turned off the alarm and propped her bike in its usual space under the stairs.

'Make yourself at home. I'll put the kettle on,' Jodie said.

Sam went into the living room. Just as he'd suspected, Jodie was into Christmas in a big way. She might not like mince pies, Christmas pud or the traditional cake, but tinsel adorned the picture-frames, cards were stuck to the walls, and there was a small Christmas tree in one corner—real, he noted with unexpected pleasure, catching its scent—hung with bronze and gold and silver stars. An angel sat at the top of the tree, and there were lights festooned over the branches, although she hadn't switched them on.

There were a couple of framed photographs on the wall—a graduation picture of a young man with fair hair and green eyes who looked so much like Jodie that he had to be her brother, and one of Jodie herself in a gown and mortar-board, sandwiched between a man and a woman with their arms proudly round her, presumably her parents. She had her mother's eyes and her father's smile, he decided. And as for her mouth...

No. He had to stop thinking about that.

More photos were dotted on the mantelpiece and festooned with tinsel, including a formal pose of a baby in a silver frame and a snapshot of Jodie holding the same baby, a milky patch on her shoulder and her face full of laughter. She'd said she had a godson, and she'd be the perfect disreputable 'auntie', no doubt teaching the little boy a stack of silly jokes as soon as he was old enough to remember the punchlines.

She looked a natural mother. She'd *be* a natural mother, he thought, and he took a step back from the mantelpiece. What on earth was he doing? He knew she wanted children one day, so he was the last person she should get involved with.

But he couldn't help himself. Moth to a flame, he thought wryly. And both of them were going to get burned, unless he managed to keep his hands off her. Maybe he should make his excuses. No socialising, no coffee, no—

'One coffee.' Jodie materialised by his side and handed him a mug of black coffee.

'Thanks.' He took a grateful sip. Maybe this would keep his mind on track.

But then she did something fatal. She closed the curtains, switched on the Christmas tree lights and turned off the overhead light. The tree was adorned with what must have been a hundred tiny white lights, which reflected off the stars to make crazy bronze and gold and silver patterns on the carpet.

He looked at the tree, he looked at the angel and he looked at Jodie. Without a word, they both placed their mugs on the low coffee-table, and he pulled her into his arms. This time, without the mistletoe and the Father Christmas outfit to give him an excuse, his lips met hers, brushing them and teasing them until he'd coaxed her mouth open, and then he kissed her properly. The way he'd wanted to on the night of the Christmas party, when she'd been in his arms and they'd both been lost in the middle of a crowd. The way he'd wanted to in the car when he'd driven her home. The way he'd finally done today…

And it was perfect. Her mouth was as sweet as he remembered, pliant against his, and she was kissing him back. Her fingers were twined in his hair, holding him to her, and he could feel her breasts swelling against his chest. The next thing he knew, he'd unbuttoned her shirt and was stroking her soft, creamy skin.

This, he thought, was heaven.

Jodie clearly felt the same, because she was unbuttoning his shirt, running her fingers over his chest. Her lips were red and swollen slightly from being kissed, her glorious hair was loose and mussed and her pupils were huge with desire.

Sam didn't dare speak, afraid of breaking the spell. Instead, he dropped to his knees and kissed his way down her body, reaching behind her at the same time to unfasten her skirt. Things went a little hazy then. The next thing he knew, they were both lying on the carpet, both naked, and every nerve in his body was screaming to be one with her.

He looked at her, all warm and soft beneath him. The lights from the tree glittered above them, making tiny patterns on her skin. She looked, he thought, like an angel. *His* angel.

Her gaze met his, and she nodded in answer to his unspoken question. He shifted slightly, and then at last he was one with her, soaring higher and higher. This was what he'd been born for, he thought. To love Jodie.

Love? The word hit him like a hammer-blow. He shouldn't be doing this. It was unprofessional, it was stupid, it was unfair to both of them—and, God help him, he couldn't stop himself. Not when the hard tips of her breasts were brushing against his chest. Not when her lips were moist and slightly parted, inviting him. Not when her body started to ripple round him, tipping him into his own release...

Jodie was seeing stars. Literally. As she looked into Sam's eyes, she could see the Christmas tree lights casting a halo round his face and their reflections in his silver-grey eyes. She wasn't a virgin—six years of being a medical student and two long relationships since graduation had put paid to that—but she'd never felt anything like this before. As if she were floating in some distant universe, where there were only the two of them and space and sparkling lights.

She shivered, and he began to move. Swiftly, she wrapped her legs round his to hold him where he was.

A slow grin lit his face. 'That, Dr Price, was an extremely wanton thing to do,' he said softly.

'Mmm.'

The grin turned to a chuckle. 'You're purring.'

'Am I?' Her voice was husky, at least an octave lower than usual, and slightly slurred from the passion they'd just shared.

'We're lying on your carpet. I'm heavy. You can't possibly be comfortable,' he pointed out.

She flexed her internal muscles and grinned wickedly as he groaned. 'I'm comfortable enough.' She tipped her head back slightly. 'Very comfortable, in fact,' she added as his body began to stir again.

'Jodie, we—'

'Shh.' She cut off the rest of his words by reaching up to kiss him.

When she'd resolved the situation to her satisfaction, their coffee was stone cold. 'I could make you another, or something,' she offered.

He stroked her face. 'Define something.'

The look in his eyes made her suddenly bold. 'My bed's a bit more comfortable than the floor.'

'Is it, now?'

'And my bath's Victorian. Large,' she said.

'Hmm.'

She nearly added, And it's Christmas. But something stopped her. Despite acting as the ward's Father Christmas that morning, Sam had made it clear that he hated Christmas. She didn't want to remind him any further. Instead, she got to her feet, bent down to take his hand and tugged.

'Pity. I was admiring the view from here,' he said.

She flushed. 'I—'

'And you blush all over. I'll have to remember that,' he added.

She led him upstairs to the bathroom. It was mainly white, with a chequerboard cushioned lino floor and a narrow, deep blue border round the walls. The bath was easily big enough for two, even a couple as tall as Sam as Jodie, and she added liberal quantities of bubble bath to the water, an expensive honey-based one Ellen bought her as an extra treat every Christmas.

Sam soaped her gently all over, arousing her with the sponge and his fingers until she was almost shivering. And then she returned the favour in spades, until he grabbed the soap from her. 'If we don't get out of this bath right now, I'll—'

'Sounds good to me, Doctor,' she teased.

'Right.' He climbed out of the bath and effortlessly hauled her out.

'Put me down! You'll give yourself a hernia!' she shrieked.

'Put you down, hmm?' And that was exactly what he did, letting her slide slowly down his body so she was left in no doubt about his feelings.

'I'd quite like to do the macho thing,' he said, 'and carry you to your room. Except I don't know where it is. And I don't think I can wait much longer.'

In answer, she smiled and twined her fingers round his.

Uncaring of the watery footprints they left on the carpet, she led him to the room at the back of the house, closed her curtains and switched on the bedside light.

She'd always preferred the space of a double bed—her idea of bliss was a lie-in on a day off, propped up with plenty of pillows, with a good book to hand, a cup of weak and very milky Earl Grey tea and soft music playing from the mini hi-fi she kept on her bedside table. Right now, she was glad of the extra space so she'd be able to lie in Sam's arms in comfort instead of them being cramped together in a single bed. And, judging by the look on his face, so was he.

'So this is your lair, Madam Spider?'

'Welcome to my parlour, Mr Fly,' she teased back.

'Indeed.' He lifted her up, pushed the duvet aside and laid her gently on the bed, then joined her. He rubbed his nose against hers. 'Well, Dr Price… Let's play!'

She chuckled, and reached up to pull his mouth back down to hers.

CHAPTER SEVEN

THE next morning, Jodie woke, stretched languidly and turned over with her eyes still closed, half expecting to curl across a warm body. But the space next to her in the bed was empty.

Frowning, she opened her eyes and sat up. She couldn't hear any noises from downstairs, so Sam obviously wasn't making coffee. And the sheet was cold enough for him to have been gone for well over an hour.

She swung her legs over the side of the bed and clambered out. She grabbed her dressing-gown from the back of the door, belted it tightly round her and checked the bathroom. Empty. She almost ran down the stairs. The kitchen was empty, too...and so was the living room.

He'd gone.

She looked round frantically, sure she'd missed something. Surely Sam wouldn't have left without a note—not after the night they'd shared? She went back upstairs. Maybe it had fallen down under a pillow, or underneath the bed... She searched frantically, but she didn't see the sticky note that had slipped down between the bed and her bedside cabinet and stuck to the wood.

He'd tidied up, she noticed—her clothes were stacked in a neat pile on the chair, instead of being the crumpled heap they'd left the night before when he'd made love to her. The two undrunk mugs of coffee had been washed up and dried, and were sitting neatly on the worktop next to the kettle. He'd drained the bath; he'd put the lid back on the bubble bath; he'd hung the towels they hadn't bothered using on the pine towel rail…

How could he have shared a night like that with her and then just tidied up and left—without a word?

Then she caught a glimpse of the clock on her microwave. It was one of the few reliable timekeepers in her house and it said half past eight. Maybe he was on duty. Maybe he'd thought she was on a late, had decided not to wake her and was going to ring her from the hospital. But she hadn't told him she was off duty, or that she was spending the next three days in Yorkshire, a five-hour drive from Melbury.

Given that it was eight-thirty now, even if she left in the next half-hour she was going to be late for lunch. Late enough for her mother to start worrying big time. She was half tempted to ring and say she'd be down tomorrow instead, but she knew everyone was expecting her. Maybe she should ring Sam and tell him where she was going. But if he was at work, he'd be right in the middle of the early rounds—and who was to say he wanted to see her anyway? Maybe he hadn't left a note because he hadn't known what to say to her. Maybe he was embarrassed about what had happened between them and regretted it.

She was certainly beginning to regret it.

Oh, what a mess. What a horrible, horrible mess. Pulling a face, she showered quickly, breakfasted and packed, then rang home to explain she'd be late before loading the boot of her elderly VW with a suitcase and a pile of presents. Finally, she checked she'd switched off all the lights, set the alarm and locked the door.

Just as Jodie drove off, the phone indoors began to ring. It continued to ring for three minutes, and then there was silence.

*   *   *

It was only when she was taking a break at a motorway service station, halfway between Norfolk and Yorkshire, that the thought hit her. She and Sam had been so absorbed in each other they hadn't even considered protection. And they'd made love more than once.

'Oh, my God!' She nearly dropped her cup of indifferent coffee. Rapidly, she did a mental calculation. Her last period had been…when?

A few days ago.

Her cycle was a bit erratic at the moment, but usually it was thirty days. Her most fertile time wouldn't be for over a week. Thank God, she wouldn't have to slope off to the chemist and buy some morning-after pills—particularly as they were at their most effective in the first twenty-four hours after unprotected sex. Today was Boxing Day and finding a chemist that was open wouldn't be easy.

Though that would be a damn sight easier than facing Sam at work. How could she talk normally to him now, remembering how his skin had felt against hers? How could she look into the eyes that she'd seen gleaming with passion and talk about observation charts and clinical symptoms and diagnoses?

Well, she'd just have to. Just like she'd spend three days with her family, as planned, and pretend nothing was wrong.

Sam was in briefly over the New Year, but somehow his path never crossed Jodie's. When he finally spoke to her, a few days later, no one would ever have known how close they'd been on Christmas Day. He'd gone back into his shell, nodding acknowledgements when he was spoken to but keeping every conversation focused solely on work. He didn't even ask anyone about their Christmas; personal details were clearly not wanted.

Mr Frosty was back with a vengeance.

Give up, Jodie told herself. He's a lost cause. And yet she couldn't help wondering why he'd suddenly withdrawn again. She'd thought before that someone must have hurt him really badly in the past, but he'd started to come out of his shell, trust people. OK, so maybe he thought he'd made a huge mistake, making love with her—but why drag everyone else into it? Unless something had happened while she'd been away. Maybe something from his past had resurfaced to haunt him. But what? And why?

There was no point in torturing herself with questions. He'd made it pretty clear that it wasn't any of her business any more—if it ever had been. From now on, it was strictly colleagues. Eventually, she'd stop wishing for something that couldn't be. She'd stop, knowing the instant he set foot in the room, even if her back was turned. She wouldn't hang around in corridors just to hear his voice.

'You're a sad case, Jodie Price,' she told herself crossly, and armed herself with her clipboard, ready to do her rounds.

Sam stared out of his office window, barely seeing what was out there. All he could think about was Jodie. Remembering her Christmas tree, how its lights had cast reflections on every surface. Including her skin.

He sighed. Jodie Price had got under his skin from the moment he'd first met her. His junior reg, who did things her way and to hell with the rules. He'd been exasperated by her—but he'd also been charmed by her impulsive kindness. The way she always stopped to talk to parents, not caring how long she spent with them, until she'd reassured them. The way she'd even tried including him in the departmental outings. And the way she'd opened herself to him on Christmas Day…

The next morning, he'd found it almost impossible to leave. All he'd wanted to do had been to curl protectively round her, hold her close to him, go back to sleep and wake her up later with a kiss. But he'd been on duty and he'd needed to check on his cat Sooty first. When he'd called her from the ward, there had been no answer. She hadn't called him. And she'd been cool and polite with him since then.

She was a bit of a scatterbrain, so she might not have seen his note—even though he'd put it on her pillow, where she'd see it when she woke—but… Oh, who was he trying to kid? Angela had told him the truth, all those years ago. He just wasn't the kind of man women wanted. Too serious, too dedicated to his work—and, worst of all, not able to give a woman the one thing she really, really wanted.

At Mario's, Jodie had been emphatic that not all women wanted children. And yet when Mick had announced he was going to be a dad and had teased her about how she'd be with her own children, she said she'd be just like any other mum. He'd seen the softness in her face as she'd talked about her future children. She wanted a boy and a girl. *One of each would be nice.*

And he couldn't even give her *one* child, let alone two.

He leaned his elbows on his desk and rested his forehead against his clenched hands. How could he go on like this, wanting her and knowing he couldn't have her? And why was he getting so obsessed with her, anyway? He'd spent just one night with her. Plenty of people had one-night stands. Hell, his profession was even renowned for it!

But Jodie wasn't 'plenty of people'.

What a mess. There was no future in a relationship with her, but on the other hand a short fling wouldn't be fair to either of them. True, the affair between them might blow over anyway, for a hundred and one different reasons—but he was beginning to have a nasty feeling that it wouldn't. Jodie reached him in a way no other woman ever had, even Angela in the early days of their marriage.

Which was why he had to do the decent thing and leave. Maybe he could go back to Liverpool, where he'd trained—it was a good five hours' drive from Melbury. Even better, back home to Cornwall, eight hours away. Or maybe he should consider working in the States. Or for a medical charity in some far-flung country, where his skills would be desperately needed and his time would be so filled that he wouldn't even have the chance to think about Jodie Price...

Until he found another job, he'd just avoid her. Then the torture would be over at last and he'd never hear so much as her name again.

A week later Sam's avoidance policy failed because he was forced to talk to Jodie about one of her patients.

'Caitlin Truman.' He sighed and looked at his watch. 'I'm due in clinic at twelve.'

'This won't take long.'

'My office?'

No way did she want to be alone with him in his office. She wanted lots of people round them to remind her to keep cool and professional instead of leaping into his arms and begging him to love her. 'I haven't had breakfast yet.'

He raised an eyebrow; it was just gone half past eleven.

'I overslept and it's been hectic on the ward,' she said, narrowing her eyes. 'My blood sugar's low.' She hadn't even had time to grab a biscuit or a cup of tea. 'I'm sure you don't want me dropping my sandwich all over your desk.'

All over his desk. A tiny tremor ran through him. He could just imagine Jodie spread over his desk, her hair loose and— No. He wasn't going to let himself remember the feel of her skin, the scent of her hair. Do that and he'd be lost. 'Canteen, then?'

'Canteen,' she agreed.

They walked down in silence—not a companionable one either. She bought a cheese salad sandwich and a bottle of fizzy water, while he stuck to a single cup of black coffee.

'Health kick?' he asked, nodding at her tray, before he could stop himself.

'Something like that.' Actually, she just didn't fancy it. 'So. Caitlin.'

He inclined his head.

'I've come across only a couple of cases of scoliosis before,' she said. 'One of them was awful—the little boy caught pneumonia and died, and there was nothing we could do about it.' She took a sip of water. 'I wanted to talk to you about the different options for Caitlin before I discussed them with her parents.'

'What have you told them so far?'

'That she has curvature of the spine—infantile idiopathic scoliosis—and nobody knows what causes the condition at the moment, though it's thought there may be some genetic involvement.' She took another sip of water and looked back at her notes. 'Some early onset curves resolve spontaneously, but Caitlin's had a second X-ray to measure the angles of the ribs to the vertebrae at the centre of the curve, and it's definitely progressive.'

'Scoliosis is actually more common than you'd think,' Sam said. 'It affects three or four children in a thousand, and one of them will need corrective surgery. If we don't treat her, she may end up being deformed and disabled in middle age.' He paused. 'Single or double curve?'

'Single—to the left, in the region of her chest.'

'How big?'

'Forty degrees.' Jodie took a bite of her sandwich. 'I know it's borderline, but it's definitely a progressive curve, so I thought surgery might be involved. If not, the curve could affect her lung function when it progresses further.'

'And she's how old?'

'Nearly two.'

Sam looked thoughtful. 'It'd be a big operation—a spinal fusion and possibly bone graft.'

'That's where you use stainless-steel rods to fix the spine and stop the curve, isn't it?'

'Yes, but the downside is having a solid spine in that area, so she won't have the full range of movement in her vertebrae.'

'What are the other options?' Jodie asked.

'Keeping a four-monthly check on her to see if it resolves. We could try physiotherapy, or we could try using a spinal brace, meaning that she'd be in plaster for a few months.'

'What do—?'

Jodie was interrupted by the sound of a chair crashing to the floor. They both looked up and, as the only doctors in the almost empty room, rushed straight over to the woman kneeling on the floor beside a small boy.

'It's my Adam—he's not breathing!' the woman cried.

Sam took one look. 'Jodie, we need adrenaline. Now!'

It would be as quick for her to run to A and E as it would be to ring them from the canteen and ask them to bring adrenaline, so Jodie took off at a rate of knots. 'Dr Jodie Price, Paediatrics,' she said, flashing her identity card at the startled receptionist. 'I need adrenaline, a syringe and a space blanket *now*—we've a case of anaphylaxis in the canteen.'

By the time she returned to the canteen, Sam had changed the boy's position on the floor, raising the child's legs to improve the flow of blood to his heart and brain. Clearly his breathing had stopped, because Sam was performing cardiopulmonary resuscitation. He'd just given Adam two breaths, and then he was back to doing cardiac compressions, pressing on the lower end of the breastbone with the heel of one hand. Fifteen of those, and then he'd give another two breaths, Jodie thought, remembering the drill. All the while, Adam's mother was looking on, her face white and her hands shaking. Slow, silent tears were rolling down her cheeks.

'Sam. Adrenaline,' Jodie said succinctly, kneeling opposite him. 'Shall I take over while you inject?'

He nodded, counting the fifteenth compression under his breath, and Jodie took over the routine of giving two breaths and fifteen compressions, while Sam injected the adrenaline.

'Come *on*, Adam. We're not going to lose you!' he muttered.

Jodie kept on with the CPR.

'There are two of us now, so I'll do the cardiac compressions while you do the breathing,' Sam directed.

It seemed to take for ever, but it could only have been a couple of minutes at most before the little boy started breathing on his own again and Sam gave him a second injection of adrenaline.

The boy's mother was weeping quietly. 'Is he going to die, Doctor?' she asked Sam.

'Not if we can help it,' Sam said.

'What's wrong with him? He— We were just sitting there and he...he just collapsed!'

'It looks as if he's had a very bad allergic reaction to something,' Sam explained. 'It's called anaphylactic shock. Has he ever reacted to anything—say, food— before? Had eczema, hay fever, asthma?'

The woman bit her lip. 'He's had a bit of a rash and swollen eyes before.'

'Do you know what caused it?' Sam asked.

The woman shook her head. 'It didn't last that long and, to be honest, I didn't really think anything of it once it had gone.'

'What was he eating just now?' Jodie asked.

'Orange juice and a biscuit.'

'May I?' Jodie gestured to the table. At the woman's nod, Jodie picked up the empty biscuit packet and glanced swiftly down the list of contents.

'It could well be peanuts,' she said, 'though we'd need to do a blood test to check.'

'Is he going to be all right?' Adam's mother asked.

The little boy's breathing was less laboured and his colour was improving, though his face was still swollen. 'I think so,' said Sam. 'We'll need to take him upstairs to the ward to keep an eye on him for a while. We might need to give him some more drugs to help him recover— at least some antihistamines to reduce the swelling.'

'We only came in to visit my mum. She's had her hip replaced. And Adam went on and on about wanting a biscuit and a drink— I brought him down here to give my mum some peace.' The woman's lower lip trembled. 'I never thought this would happen!'

Sam was busy checking the boy's pulse and respiration. Jodie glanced at him, then decided to reassure Adam's mother herself. 'It's fairly frightening to watch,' she said, putting an arm round the woman's shoulders. 'Sorry, I haven't asked you your name yet.' She smiled. 'I guess we were a bit preoccupied.'

'Mrs Kinnerton. Mandy Kinnerton.'

'I'm Jodie Price and this is Sam Taylor,' Jodie said. 'What's happened to Adam is that his body's immune system has overreacted a bit. It's as if his body thinks whatever he's eaten is dangerous, so it releases all sorts of chemicals to repel the ''invader'' and protect the body. Those chemicals sometimes cause a rash and swollen eyes in a mild reaction; in a stronger reaction, like the one Adam's just had, his throat and mouth swell up as well, so he has problems breathing, and his blood vessels widen and so his blood pressure drops. Did he say he felt dizzy, too?'

'He just said he didn't feel very well and...down he went.' Mandy Kinnerton was still shaking.

'When he ate whatever gave him the rash before, did he say his mouth tingled or itched?' Jodie asked.

'I—I can't remember.'

'It's all right,' Jodie soothed. 'We'll sort it all out. Dr Taylor—' again, she avoided the Dr—Mr explanation '—gave Adam some adrenaline. It's a hormone the body produces, too—it makes the heart beat faster. The adrenaline we've given him will make his blood vessels go back to normal, relax the muscles in his lungs again to help him breathe, and stop the swelling around his face and lips.'

'And all this happened just because he's eaten some-

thing with peanuts in?' Mandy Kinnerton looked at Jodie
in disbelief.

'It's just a guess,' Jodie said, 'but peanuts are one of
the most common causes of allergies—around one in two
hundred children react to peanuts, though not all of them
react quite as strongly as this. Up on the ward, we'll
check him over thoroughly and ask you a few more questions, if you don't mind, to find out a bit more about any
problems Adam's had in the past and whether he has
asthma, hay fever, that sort of thing. Then we'll take a
blood test to check what caused his reaction. If I'm right
and it *is* peanuts, you'll need to make sure Adam doesn't
eat them again, in any form.'

'Not ever?'

'Not ever,' Jodie repeated. 'You'll need to check the
labels of everything for peanuts—even peanut oil, so
you'll have to be careful when you eat out, too, in case
the food's been cooked with peanut oil. In some cases,
you might find he has a reaction if he even touches whatever he's allergic to, let alone eats it— I've known cases
where someone's eaten peanuts and kissed someone who
reacts to them, whose eyes swelled up immediately.'

'It— Could this happen again?'

'Hopefully not, though we can show you what to do
if it does. We'll be able to give you an adrenaline pen
so you don't have to worry about syringes—it's really
easy to use, and you can get practice pens so Adam can
have a go on an orange and won't waste the drugs. We'll
show both you and Adam how to use it, and you'll need
to tell everyone at school and his friends' parents, so they
know what to watch out for and can use the adrenaline
pen straight away if he does have another reaction.'

'But he is going to be all right?'

'He'll be fine,' Sam said. 'A bit scared after what's

happened and he'll want a big cuddle from his mum, but he'll be fine. We'll just get him up to the children's ward, and Dr Price will sit with you while we admit him.'

'You saved his life,' Mandy said. 'I don't know how I'm ever going to thank you.'

Sam shrugged. 'It's our job.'

She frowned for a moment and then her face cleared. 'Do you work on the children's ward?'

Jodie smiled. 'We do, indeed. We're probably the best people you could have sat near, except for someone from A and E.'

'Thank you. From the bottom of my heart. And no more biscuits for you, my lad.' The sternness of her last words was belied by the slight tremor in her voice.

'Mum…' The little boy reached out for his mother's hand.

'It's all right, Adam. We'll soon have you feeling well again,' Jodie said comfortingly. 'And your mum can stay with you as long as she likes.'

To her surprise, Sam accompanied them back to the ward. Just as he was about to leave again, Jodie excused herself from Adam and his mother for a moment.

'We need to talk,' she said quietly.

He nodded. 'About Caitlin Truman.'

'Not just Caitlin.'

'I don't think there's anything to talk about.'

She flushed. 'I disagree. What about…?' She couldn't quite bring herself to say the words. *What about us?*

Clearly, he guessed what she'd been about to say, because he sighed heavily. 'All right. But not here. And I'm in clinic now.'

'When, then?'

'After clinic. Two?'

She nodded. 'In the canteen?'

He shook his head. 'Take a late lunch. I'll meet you by the river.'

In public—and yet somewhere far more private than Melbury City General. Somewhere they wouldn't be overheard and gossip wouldn't start flying round. 'Two.' She nodded, and turned back to see to Adam and his mother.

CHAPTER EIGHT

AT A quarter to two, Jodie headed through the centre of Melbury, trying to avoid the mass of shoppers laden with New Year bargains. It was dry but it was much colder than she'd realised and she shoved her hands deep in the pockets of her woollen coat, wishing that she'd remembered her scarf as well. There was no time to go back for it, though—not if she wanted to meet Sam at two. As it was, she was cutting it fine.

By the river. That could mean anywhere from the bottom of the cathedral close through to the bridge by the train station or even by the ruined fourteenth-century walls. She really should have pinned him down to an exact place.

As she walked down the close, she heard the cathedral clock's melancholy tune and then the hour strike. Two o'clock. Well, Sam knew she was always late. He'd wait for a couple more minutes—wouldn't he?

At the bottom of the cathedral close, she turned left. Luckily, her hunch was right, because eventually she saw him sitting on the wooden bench by the old city walls. He looked tense to the point of being rigid. She'd bet his neck and shoulders ached, but there was no point in suggesting doing something about it. The way Sam was right now, he'd refuse to let her touch him, even impersonally.

Not that she could be impersonal where Sam was concerned. Not now she knew what it felt like to sleep in his arms.

He'd chosen to meet her at a place that always gave

her the creeps, even in the middle of summer. On a winter's afternoon, it was even spookier, the flints pitch black against the sky and the tops of the old towers now crumbled, leaving the insides open to the elements. Looking up through one of the towers of the old city walls was like being in a deep, dark hole from which you knew you'd never escape. But she supposed the place suited Sam's mood: cold and lonely and remote.

'Sorry I'm late,' she said as she reached him.

He shrugged. 'It's not important.'

She sat down beside him. He didn't move a muscle; she sighed inwardly. She was going to have to broach the subject. But how? *When we made love*—well, it hadn't been love on his part, had it? *When we had sex*—no. That made it sound cheap, nasty and meaningless, and it had been far from that. *When we…* What was the point of beating about the bush? If the silence between them stretched on any longer, she'd scream.

'Christmas Day. We didn't use protection,' she said quietly.

He nodded. 'It doesn't matter.'

She stared at him. Was he trying to say that if *he* had made her pregnant, he didn't care? 'Doesn't it bother you that there might be consequences?'

'There won't be.'

'I don't understand.' Her eyes widened. Was he suggesting she should have a termination? But the man who treated children on the ward with such care couldn't possibly want her to get rid of a baby he saw only as an encumbrance—could he? Her stomach clenched. If she was pregnant with his child, she couldn't just snuff out a life and put it down to mere carelessness. Yes, it would be hard, especially if Sam decided he wanted nothing to do with the baby, but she'd keep it.

'Sam, surely you don't—?'

'I guarantee it,' he cut in. 'You're definitely not pregnant, Jodie.'

Was he trying to tell her that he'd had a vasectomy years back? Or was it something else? The bleakness in his eyes made her shiver inwardly. She couldn't begin to imagine what sort of hell he was going through right now. If only he'd let her close enough to take the pain away. 'She must have hurt you very much,' she said softly.

His face hardened. 'Have you been asking questions about me?'

'No. Just making an educated guess,' she said succinctly.

He massaged his temples. 'Sorry. I'm a little...touchy on the subject.' He sighed. 'I owe you an explanation. Jodie, you want a baby, right?'

'No! I'm only twenty-eight,' she protested.

'Not necessarily right now,' he said. 'I mean, at some time in the future, you'll want to have a baby.'

'Probably. Yes.' Surely he wasn't worried about the age difference? He was only six or seven years older than she was. They had plenty of time. 'What's that got to do with us?'

'Everything.' Sam closed his eyes. 'I can't have children, Jodie. Ever.'

So *that* was why he was so *blasé* now about what had happened between them on Christmas Day. He'd known then that there was no chance of her falling pregnant—even if she'd been at the most fertile part of her cycle.

And then it hit her. Sam couldn't have children. So not only was she definitely not pregnant now, but if she spent her life with Sam she'd never have children of her own. Never walk round the supermarket with her hand resting protectively on the top of her bump; never shop together for a cot and a pram and tiny, soft baby clothes; never hold their baby son with Sam's eyes and his slow, sweet smile; never see their little girl pulling herself up on the furniture, gurgling as her father cheered her on and clapped with pride.

Right now, her career was her main focus; but somehow Jodie had always assumed that one day she'd have children, compromising with her partner so she could still work part time but also bring the children up herself and see their first steps, hear their first words, be there to comfort them after a bump or a scrape.

Suddenly, that was no longer an option.

There wasn't a compromise any more, but a choice. Sam or children.

'Y-you can't have children,' she repeated numbly, hoping she'd misheard.

His expression grew bleak. 'Angela was right. I'm not husband material, Jodie. Never was, never will be.'

'Angela?'

'My wife. Ex-wife,' he amended heavily, his shoulders sagging.

She waited, hoping that he'd explain. But he'd retreated back into his shell and was just sitting there on the bench, his face tortured and his eyes despairing. If she said the wrong thing now, she'd never learn the truth. Much as she wanted to yell at him and beat her fists on his chest and do something—anything—to make him stop throwing away their future together, she knew she had to go carefully. The back of her neck felt hot with fear and her hands were shaking. She laced her fingers together and hoped he hadn't noticed the tremors.

'Sam,' she said softly. 'I—I don't understand.'

His face twisted. 'It's not something I talk about.'

Did he think she didn't realise that? She bit back the sharp words. 'Sam. You've—I realise you've been hurt in the past,' she said carefully, stumbling over the words, 'but it doesn't have to be that way. Not with me.'

'Forget me, Jodie. I can't give you a future.'

'I— Sam, I don't want to hurt you, but I...I need to know.'

'All the sordid details?' he asked nastily.

She flinched. 'No. That's not what I meant.'

He closed his eyes. 'I'm sorry. It's just every time I think I—' He stopped abruptly and took a deep breath. 'I had an undescended testicle as a child, and my mother was too embarrassed to talk to the doctor about it, so I didn't have surgery to correct it. I had it removed in my late teens, but it was too late. Angela wanted a baby but...' He shrugged. 'We had the tests and I can't have children.'

Jodie desperately wanted to reach out to him and hold him, but his body language was screaming at her to keep off. 'Oh, Sam, I'm so sorry.' If only his mother had talked to their doctor. Most cases of undescended testicles resolved themselves naturally by around three or four months of age; nowadays, they could be treated by twice-weekly injection of human chorionic gonadotropin, the hormone that stimulated the maturation of the testicles and caused them to move down over the course of several weeks. If that didn't work, surgery was an option. Sometimes there was a hernia accompanying the undescended testicle which needed to be fixed. But if the undescended testicle was left in place, it lost the cells that made sperm, leading to fertility problems and a higher risk of cancer.

'After the test results came back, things were bad between us. It wasn't Angela's fault. I— Well, you know what they call me on the ward. Mr Frosty. I knew how desperately she wanted a baby. I wanted one myself. But I didn't know how to stop us both hurting, so I buried myself in work. I used to work late so I wouldn't have to face her—or the fact I was a failure as a husband. I didn't know what to say to her and I...' His voice cracked. 'I couldn't talk about it. I couldn't comfort her. I couldn't give her what she needed most. So...'

He didn't have to say any more. It was obvious: Angela had left him. 'Sam, it takes two to make a marriage.' And to break it. She reached out to take his hand. 'It's not *all* your fault.'

'Jodie, it's pointless discussing it. I'm not the man you need.' His voice was cold and clipped.

He was hurting as much as she was, she was sure. And she knew she had to be the one to reach out— Sam was way too proud. She didn't dare voice the L-word—she didn't think he could handle it right now—but she couldn't just walk away, letting him think she didn't care. 'Supposing I think you're the one I want to spend my life with?' she asked.

'Then you're mistaken. Very much mistaken.' A muscle clenched in his jaw. 'You adore children.'

'That's why I'm a paediatrician.' And why he was one, too, she'd bet her last penny. He hadn't said as much, but she guessed he'd gone into paediatrics after he'd found out about his infertility.

'It's more than that. I've seen you on the ward, feeding babies and cuddling them and singing them lullabies and playing with the bigger ones—all way beyond your job description. You even do it when you're supposed to be off duty.'

'OK, so I love children.' She shrugged. 'So what?'

'Jodie, you said you wanted children. One of each, you

said. Back at the revue,' he reminded her. 'And I can't give you a child. Ever.' He shook his head in frustration. 'Don't you understand? Whatever you feel about me now—whatever I feel about you—one day, you'll wake up and you'll want a baby. A baby I can't give you. It's corrosive, Jodie, the need for a baby. It burns everything in its path. It'll become the most important thing in your life and you'll grow to hate me because I can't give you what you want.'

'No, I won't.'

Yes, she would. He'd already lived through it once—and he couldn't do it again. He couldn't spend the rest of his life waiting and hoping and praying she wouldn't want a baby and resent him for denying her one, and every day growing more and more scared. Every day knowing that they were getting closer and closer to the point where she'd realise what she was missing out on.

The rainy November look was back in his eyes as he stared at her. 'Can you look me in the eye and tell me it doesn't matter if you don't have children—*ever*?'

'I...' Jodie fell silent. Could she? Right now, she wanted Sam more than she'd ever wanted anything in her whole life. But was it enough—for both of them? Eventually, she sighed. 'I don't know, Sam. I need time to think about it.'

'Exactly. And when you do, you'll realise I'm right. You need someone who can give you what you want.'

Jodie shook her head. 'That's not what I meant. I mean I need time to come to terms with it—I'd always thought I'd have kids.' She swallowed. 'But if we can't, we can't. Whatever happens, we'll still have each other.'

'And you'll miss out on the feeling of your baby growing inside you, the first kick, seeing it move at the scan and hearing its heartbeat on the Sonicaid. Then the mo-

ment when you first look at your newborn and realise
what a miracle you've brought into the world, then seeing
your baby grow up—the first smiles and the first steps
and hearing the first words and all the silly, funny things
small children say. I can't make you lose all that.'

'It's my choice,' Jodie pointed out. 'And if I choose
you—'

'You'll regret it,' he cut in. 'Not now, maybe not tomorrow—but, believe me, the day will come when you'll
have this yearning, this hollow in your heart that nothing
else can fill.' He didn't even realise he was speaking—
the words just forced themselves out as he thought about
what had happened all those years ago. 'You won't be
able to stop thinking about it. It'll be a physical need.
Every time you see someone with a baby, you'll start to
shrivel inside, because you know you'll never have that.
You'll start asking yourself, Why you? Why can they
have a baby and you can't? Every time you see a mother
telling off her kids, you'll want to march over and shake
her, tell her she should damn well appreciate what she
has, because you'd give anything to be in her shoes.'

'How do you know?' she demanded.

*Because that's what happened with Angela and I
couldn't bear it to happen with you.* The words stuck in
his throat. 'I just do,' he forced out.

She stared at him. 'So you're going to give up on us,
just like that?'

'There is no "us".'

She laughed shortly. 'So you're telling me Christmas
Day didn't happen?'

'God, help me, it did,' he said hoarsely. 'I'm a selfish
bastard, Jodie. I should have left you alone, but I—I just
couldn't resist you. I tried, believe me I tried. I kept telling myself that you were off limits.'

Well, that explained why he'd blown hot and cold on her. Wanting her, reacting with his body—then thinking about it and deciding he couldn't offer her enough so he should stay away from her.

'But once I'd touched you I couldn't help myself. I wanted you so much.'

'You're selfish, all right,' Jodie said. All the anger and hurt and frustration she'd felt since Christmas Day came boiling out. 'Woke up in the morning with second thoughts, did you?'

'What?'

'Christmas Day. If you had time to tidy up, you had time to scribble a note.'

He frowned. 'I *did* leave you a note.'

'Where? Planet Taylor?' she asked nastily.

'On the pillow. Next to you,' he said.

'Saying what, exactly? Wham, bam, thank you, ma'am?'

'No. That I was on early, I needed to check my cat was OK and I didn't want to wake you. I said I'd ring you.'

'Oh, yes?'

'Yes.' He paused. 'And I did, later that morning. You didn't answer.'

'I'd gone to my parents' in Yorkshire.'

They looked at each other for a moment.

'Jodie, I wouldn't have just walked out. Not after...' His voice tailed off.

She nodded slowly. 'So you admit that what happened between us was special?'

He raked a hand through his hair. 'That isn't the point.'

'Isn't it? It wasn't just you, remember. It was *me*, too. I wanted you, Sam. I wanted to make love with you.'

'It was just sex.'

'Like hell it was!' She could tell from the colour of
his eyes that he hadn't meant it. He was just trying to
put her off him because he was too stubborn to believe
she wanted him for himself.

'OK, so it wasn't just sex,' he admitted. 'But we didn't
use protection. Doesn't that tell you anything?' He
twisted his fingers together in anguish. 'If my condition
was different, you could be carrying my child right now.'

Just for a moment, she saw sheer, naked longing in his
eyes. Sam wanted a baby, the baby that could never be.
And she also knew he'd rather die than admit it. 'It was
a safe time of the month,' she said lightly.

'And you knew that at the time?'

For a moment she was tempted to lie. She flushed.
'I...um, wasn't even thinking about it. Not right then.'
Protection had been the last thing on her mind. All she'd
been aware of had been Sam, and how much she'd
wanted to make love with him.

'Exactly. If you were determined *not* to have a baby,
you'd have made sure one of us used protection. What
we did was irresponsible.'

'Oh, for God's sake! We got carried away—what does
that say about us? Just that we're human. OK, we're doctors and we should have known better, but...' She glowered. 'And if you're thinking of STDs, Sam—'

'Of course I'm not!'

She ignored him. 'I don't make a habit of bed-hopping
and I don't think you do either. You're making too much
of this.'

'I don't want your pity and I don't need it,' he said
tightly.

'I'm not pitying you!' she yelled back. Didn't he realise she loved him?

'Jodie, it's not going to work out. Just forget me. I'll be gone soon.'

'What do you mean, gone?'

He stood up. 'What I said. Gone.' He started to walk away.

She ran after him. 'Sam Taylor, don't you *dare* walk away from me! What do you mean, gone?'

'I'm applying for another job.'

'Where?'

'Does it matter?'

'Of course it matters!'

He stopped abruptly. 'Jodie, I'm leaving Melbury—for your sake as well as mine. Don't make this any harder than it has to be.'

'Sam—'

'We've said everything there is to say. One day, when you're happily married with children, you'll remember this moment and you'll know I'm doing the right thing. We don't have a future, Jodie. End of story. Goodbye.'

This time, when he walked away, Jodie stayed where she was, her eyes blurred by tears. She'd put her heart on the line, told him that she wanted to spend her future with him, and he'd rejected her.

Somehow, she had to get through the rest of the afternoon at the hospital. She only hoped she didn't have to consult Sam about a patient today. They hadn't finished their discussion about Caitlin Truman, but maybe she'd manage to persuade the consultant's secretary to arrange an appointment for the Trumans to see Sam directly. And she'd cope with Sam herself *after* today.

Steeling herself, she stood up and trudged back through the cathedral. She heard the mournful five-note chimes that heralded the first quarter hour. A quarter past two. Had it really been just fifteen minutes ago that she'd come hurrying to meet Sam, full of hope that they could sort everything out? It felt like a lifetime away. And the rest of her life stretched out before her, grey and empty without him.

CHAPTER NINE

SAM was nowhere to be seen that afternoon, and Jodie was grateful to leave at the end of her shift. She cycled home wearily, until the blast of a car horn made her realise she'd been distracted enough to swerve off the cycle lane and into the path of the traffic behind her. Shakily, she dismounted and walked her bike the rest of the way home, to be safe.

Life without Sam. It was unthinkable. When she'd thought he'd dumped her without a word, it had been bad enough. But now she knew the truth, that he was ending it between them all because of her biological clock— which hadn't even started ticking yet—it was unbearable.

When she got home, she rushed upstairs to check the bedroom for the note he'd left her at Christmas. This time she searched the room more thoroughly and discovered the sticky note attached to the bedside cabinet, hidden by the frame of her bed. Obviously she'd dislodged it from the pillow in her sleep.

Her eyes pricked with tears as she read it. 'I'm on earlies and you looked too peaceful to wake! I'm going home to check on the cat and I'll ring you later this morning. Happy Christmas. Sam.'

'Happy Christmas.' This from the man who'd admitted how much he hated Christmas.

Happy Christmas.

It was as near as Sam Taylor would get to a declaration of love.

Back then, he'd been prepared to give it a go. If only

she'd found the note. If only she hadn't gone to Yorkshire. If only she'd phoned him on the ward, not caring about what the grapevine would make of it... Maybe then they'd have had a chance.

Now he'd made the decision for them both. Jodie sat on the edge of her bed, drawing her knees up to her chin and wrapping her arms round her legs. Would she really have such a desperate need for a baby that she'd grow to hate him? Would anger and hurt and frustration and resentment replace the longing for his touch? Would they end up trapped in a silent hell of a relationship, where neither dared voice their feelings and both worked late to avoid seeing the other? Was it really a stark choice between having the man she loved and having babies? Was there no compromise, no in-between that would make them both happy?

She shivered. Right now, what she wanted was Sam. She wanted to feel his arms round her, his mouth against hers, his voice whispering in her ear that everything was going to be all right, that they'd find a way to work things out. Together. She wanted to smell his warm, masculine scent; she wanted his skin sliding across hers as he made love with her; she wanted...

But she had a nasty feeling that she was wishing for what she couldn't have.

The next morning, after a sleepless night, Jodie still couldn't answer the questions. Would she want a baby more than anything else? Right now, she couldn't imagine it. But the yearning, the need she felt for Sam, wanting to touch him and hold him and kiss him and lose herself in his body—would the longing for a baby be as strong?

She couldn't predict the future. Nobody could. But if

they didn't give it a try, they'd never know. The problem was trying to convince Sam of that. Stubborn didn't even begin to describe him. And she wasn't sure she was ever going to be able to change his mind.

When she walked onto the ward, she felt sick, but she knew she had to face Sam some time. Maybe if she could make Sam see how well they worked together as colleagues, he wouldn't leave. And then maybe she'd be able to thaw him out again, take it step by step, persuade him to give them a chance.

Then she remembered his parting words to her. *We don't have a future, Jodie. End of story. Goodbye.* What could be more final than that?

She took a deep breath. Well, she'd just have to be professional about it. He was her colleague—albeit not for that much longer—and their patients shouldn't suffer because of that.

'Isn't Caitlin Truman your patient?' Julianne, Sam's secretary, asked pointedly when Jodie asked her to set up an appointment for the Trumans to see Sam.

'Yes.'

'Then shouldn't *you* be speaking to them about this?'

Jodie knew that the woman was only trying to do her job—juggle the demands on the consultant's time—but Julianne, despite being only twenty-five, was the archetypal dragon secretary. She even dressed the part, with her hair scraped back severely, little black suits and glasses that just happened to slide down her nose so she could glare over them at any doctor who dared question her authority.

'The parents need information that I don't have and Mr Taylor does,' Jodie said calmly, just about managing to quell the urge to snap at Julianne. It wasn't the secretary's fault that she and Sam had reached an impasse.

'I just feel it's better for them to go higher than me so I want to refer them up.'

'Hmm.' Julianne looked at the computer screen and tutted. 'I'm afraid Mr Taylor's very busy.'

Jodie dug her nails into her palm, but it didn't stop her reacting to the patronising tone. 'Caitlin Truman is potentially a very sick little girl.'

Julianne's lips thinned. 'I can't work miracles, you know.'

'What's the problem?' a voice asked behind them.

Damn. Why had her early warning signal failed her? Jodie wondered crossly. Or maybe that was a good sign. Maybe she was starting the long, long healing process to get over him. She steeled herself and turned to face Sam. 'The Trumans would like to see you,' she said. 'I thought it might be better to transfer Caitlin from my list to yours.'

'I see.'

He really wasn't going to make this easy for her, was he? she fumed inwardly. He could at least do his bit. 'Of course,' she said sweetly, 'I realise you're much too busy to ask you to use this as a teaching case. That's why I've asked Julianne to schedule an appointment for you with the Turners. I'm bowing out.'

If Sam could have waved a magic wand and whisked his secretary to the ends of the earth—if only temporarily—at that moment, he would have done so. He was standing so close to Jodie that he could smell the honey-scented bubble bath they'd used together on Christmas Day. Her face was composed and she sounded completely professional, but her eyes were sending him a completely different message. She was itching to slap his face. Or possibly worse.

He'd been cruel to be kind. If only she knew how much he wanted to touch her. How he wanted to pull her into his arms, hold her close, breathe in that honey scent and feel the softness of her skin against his. How he wanted to kiss her, feel her lips soften under his and part, letting him deepen the intimacy. How he wanted to lose himself in her body, take them both to paradise and beyond.

But it wasn't fair. He could never give Jodie the child she wanted. Right now, she was concentrating on her career. But in five years? Ten? He couldn't go through all that again. Month after month of her trying to pretend not to mind that she wasn't pregnant—month after month of her gradually withdrawing from him, until their marriage was nothing but an empty shell. It wasn't fair to either of them. He had to do it this way until he found another job and they had enough distance between them to forget each other.

Not that he thought he'd ever be able to forget her. She'd haunt his dreams for the rest of his life. Dreams of Jodie, wide-eyed and laughing because she'd felt the little bubbly sensation of the baby's first kick. Dreams of resting his hand on the bump and feeling his baby kick inside her. Dreams of Jodie and a little girl with his dark hair and her green eyes—or a little boy with a mop of blond curls and grey eyes.

Dreams that could never, ever become real.

'Julianne, could you try to fit the Trumans in some time during the next week, please?' he asked.

Julianne gave Jodie a look of sheer dislike, no doubt expecting to see triumph in the young doctor's eyes. But there was no triumph there, Sam realised when he also glanced at Jodie as she muttered her thanks before walking away. Just a dullness, a blunting of her usual enthusiasm. And he knew he was responsible. Yet another reason why he should leave. How could he live with himself if he'd taken away all the pleasure in her professional life, too?

'You're getting as bad as old Frosty-boy,' Duncan, one of the junior doctors, complained a few days later.

'What?' Jodie glared at him.

'Either it's catching or you've got the worst case of PMT I've ever come across.'

'Oh, grow up, Duncan,' she snapped.

'Ooh! Keep your hair on, Jo-jo.'

'There's nothing wrong,' she said tightly.

'If you say so.' He shrugged. 'But you used to be the life and soul of the party. You haven't been to Mario's with us for ages and you never seem to laugh any more. Paeds used to be hard work but fun. Now it's just hard work.'

It won't be for much longer, Jodie thought. Sam's going to leave. And as for me…I don't even know if I want to stay in medicine any more. She shrugged and turned away.

Duncan came over to sit on the chair next to hers. 'Jo-jo, are you all right?' he asked, frowning in concern and clearly regretting the way he'd teased her. 'I mean, I haven't seen you smile for days. It isn't—you haven't had some bad news or anything?'

Bad news. Yeah, you could say that, she thought. The man I love won't take a chance with me. He thinks he knows what's best for us, even though he doesn't, and soon I'm never going to see him again. 'Nothing's wrong,' she lied. 'Just rushed off my feet, trying to sort that paper out…' The paper she'd finished days ago. 'I wish I'd never started it, to be honest.' And she wasn't talking about the paper.

'All work and no p-l-a-y,' Duncan said, spelling it out in phonetics.

She smiled, despite her inner misery. 'Oh, you.'

Duncan smiled back, clearly relieved at seeing his colleague acting more like her usual self. 'Tell you what. I'll cook you dinner tonight, to cheer you up.'

'*You'll* cook?' she asked, shocked. Duncan's culinary skills were reputedly on a par with her own.

'OK, if you don't fancy mushy beans on burned toast, I'll take you out for a pizza,' he suggested. 'Or a Chinese. How about an Indian? Whatever you want. You choose.'

Sam, who'd been about to walk into the room, abruptly turned and walked away as he heard Duncan's words. Yes, he knew that Jodie should find herself someone else—but he couldn't face hearing her accept a date with another man. His self-control wasn't that strong.

It was to face a much harder test within the next two hours.

'Come in,' he called at the slightly timid rap on his door.

When Jodie walked in, it was a full minute before he could speak. He pretended to be finalising some notes while he composed himself. 'Yes, Dr Price?' he asked hoarsely.

She placed a bottle of champagne on his desk. 'From the Kinnertons.'

'The little boy with anaphylaxis?'

She nodded. 'They've had the test results back and it's definitely peanuts. The allergy team's given them a list of things to watch out for and taught them how to use an Epipen. Anyway, his mum just brought this in.' Her voice cracked. 'She said we could share it. I... You did the hard part. I thought you should have it.'

As she turned away, he said neutrally, 'Take it, Jodie. You work hard enough. Perhaps you could share it with Duncan tonight.'

She whipped round. 'What?'

'Aren't you going out with him?'

She stared at him in disbelief. 'How can you even *ask* that?'

'I heard him invite you out.'

Her eyes widened as she digested the message. His voice was neutral but his eyes were far from it: they were a stormy, angry grey. Sam was actually jealous! For the first time in days, a real smile curved her lips. 'Since you were eavesdropping, you should have waited a bit longer, Sam. You'd have heard me refuse. Anyway, I think of Duncan more as the kid brother I never had than anything else.'

'It's really none of my business,' Sam said, backtracking swiftly.

'Isn't it?' Jodie looked at him, noting the high colour slashing across his cheekbones. 'We've been avoiding each other for days—and it's not going to work.'

'How do you mean?'

There were deep shadows under his eyes, too, as if he hadn't slept. As if he'd lain awake night after night, wanting to feel her beside him. Wanting to kiss her, touch her, make love with her, lose himself in the comfort of her body. 'We feel the same way,' she said quietly.

'No, we don't.'

'Prove it,' she challenged.

His eyes narrowed. 'How?'

She circumnavigated his desk and stood beside him. Then she reached out to cup his face. 'If we don't, then it won't bother you if I…' Swiftly, she bent forward and touched her lips to his. Gentle, soft, tiny butterfly kisses.

Sam had intended to stay completely calm and neutral, but his body had other ideas. Before he knew it, he'd pulled her onto his lap, her soft curls were wound round his fingers, and his mouth was urgently, desperately covering hers. The sweetness of her mouth was like a drug, and he wanted more. Much, much more.

Jodie was kissing him back and her fingers were tangled in his hair, urging him on. Sam lost himself in the pleasure of touching her, holding her again. She smelled so good and her skin was so soft, so sweet—he wanted to taste every centimetre of her.

One hand slid under her loose top and his fingertips brushed the skin on her midriff. She arched against him and he unclipped her bra, then moved round to caress the hardening peaks of her breasts. She made a small murmur of pleasure, and he lost it completely. He pushed her top up and bent to suckle one breast. Jodie's fingers were tangled in his hair, urging him on. He turned his attention to the other breast, and Jodie sighed.

'Sam. I need you. Please. Now.' And at least they didn't have to stop because they didn't have a condom, she thought. She didn't want to give Sam the chance to think about what they were doing. If she could get him to follow his heart instead of his head, maybe he'd realise how much she loved him and they could face their future together.

Completely forgetting where he was, and incredibly turned on by the huskiness in her voice, he swept the papers from his desk with one arm, lifted her onto the bare wood and knelt between her thighs.

Jodie sighed with pleasure as he entered her, and wrapped her legs round his waist, drawing him deeper. She cupped his head and gently drew his face down to hers, rubbing her nose against his and then kissing him deeply. Lost and helpless, Sam reacted to her need, deepening his thrusts. His senses were filled by her—the honey-eyed scent of her skin, the sound of her breathing, the feel of her skin against his, the taste of her mouth under his own—and the sheer, mind-numbing pleasure in her wide green eyes as she reached her climax and held his gaze with her own.

'I love you,' he murmured against her mouth as he fell into the whirlpool of his own release.

A long, long time later, when their heartbeats had slowed down to normal, Sam's mind snapped back into place. They were still entwined, spread across his desk, Jodie's hair fanning out around her just as he'd imagined it. She was stroking his hair—and he was still kissing her, as if his mouth couldn't get enough of hers. And, worse still, he'd just admitted that everything she'd said was true. He'd told her he loved her—even though he knew it was unfair and she deserved better than him.

Where the hell was his self-control when he needed it?

Horrified by his selfishness, he pulled back and restored a rough semblance of order to Jodie's clothes, then his own. Anyone could have seen them making love over his desk. And anyone who walked in right now would know exactly what they'd been doing. Her hair was a mess, her lips were reddened and swollen with arousal, her eyes were glittering and her clothes—despite his best efforts—were distinctly disordered. Heaven alone knew what he looked like. Probably just as bad.

He slumped back into his chair. How on earth was he going to sort out this mess? Where was he going to start? 'Jodie, I'm sorry,' he said softly.

She sat up on the edge of his desk, crossing one leg over the other, and grinned. 'Nothing to apologise for. Sam, you want me as much as I want you. What we just did—'

'Was completely unprofessional,' he cut in. 'We're in my office, for God's sake! Anyone could have walked in.'

'I know that. You know that.' She spread her hands. 'And it didn't stop us, did it?'

'No.' He thrust a shaking hand through his hair. 'And we didn't use protection.'

She smiled wryly. 'No need, is there? And we've already established that neither of us bed-hops.'

'Jodie, what happened—it was completely irresponsible of me.'

'And me,' she cut in. 'We were there *together*, Sam. All the way.'

All the way. He wanted her again, so desperately. He wanted to lock the door and make love to her again until neither of them could even think straight, let alone speak.

But he couldn't. He had to do what was best for her. He shook his head. 'We can't do this, Jodie.'

'Yes, we can. We just need to talk.'

'No. You can't throw your future away like this,' he said doggedly.

'It's my future. So it's my decision,' she pointed out. 'I want you—kids or no kids.' She gave him a confident smile—the young doctor Sam knew so well from work, ready to battle the world and argue her case when she thought she was right.

But this time he couldn't let her win. For her own sake. Somehow he had to get through to her and make her understand what she was proposing to give up. 'Jodie, I've seen the way you are with the kids on the ward. Don't you want to give that love and support to your own child, too? See the first smile, the first steps, hear your baby call you Mummy?'

'Sam, I...'

The hesitation was enough to tell him the truth. Whatever she felt for him, she wanted a baby. A baby he couldn't give her. 'You do. I know you do, Jodie—and you've got so much love to give. I can't let you sacrifice that,' he said softly.

'Then what do we do? Stay apart, both miserable?'

'It'll pass,' Sam said. It would take a long, long time, but one day he'd wake up and he'd stop wanting her. Stop loving her.

And it was precisely because he loved her that he knew he had to give up that love.

'Have you never heard of compromise? There are treatments for infertility, you know!'

He shook his head. 'Not where this is concerned. And if we carry on, we'll both end up hurt.' God only knew why he was talking about future hurt. It already felt like he was slowly bleeding to death, knowing he had to leave her. 'I'm sorry, Jodie. But you're young—you'll get over it. You'll meet someone else, someone who can give you what you want.'

Jodie stared at him for a long, long moment. He thought she was going to argue, but she said nothing—just looked at him. Her eyes were still glittering, but this time with the beginning of tears instead of passion.

'All right, Sam. You've made your point. I give up,' she said quietly, and left the room.

Every nerve in his body screamed to him to go after her, to pull her back into his arms and tell her it was OK, he loved her, he wanted her and somehow they'd make it together.

'Listening to my heart got me into this mess in the first place,' he muttered under his breath. 'I've got to stay away from her—for her own good.'

CHAPTER TEN

IT'LL PASS. Jodie told herself that every time she heard Sam's voice in the middle of ward rounds, every time she had to deal politely and neutrally with him, when all she really wanted to do was to fling herself in his arms and beg him to take a chance.

But two days later, on her day off when she was at Ellen's house, watching *Sleeping Beauty* and eating more than her fair share of the chocolate buttons Ellen had sneaked out of the fridge while Billy slept, she burst into tears. The song about walking with your true love once upon a dream was just too much for her—because that was all she had now. Dreams of what might have been.

Ellen immediately folded her in her arms and let her cry. Finally, Jodie stifled her sobs. 'I'm sorry.'

'I'm your best mate. That's what I'm for.' Ellen gave her a hug. 'It's Sam, isn't it?'

Jodie nodded, and told Ellen the full story.

When she'd finished, Ellen whistled. 'He's stubborn, I'll give him that. But he has a point, Jodie. Remember how I swore I wouldn't have kids until I was at least thirty and had made deputy head?'

'Yeah.'

'And now look at me. Twenty-eight, with a toddler, and I've gone back part time because I couldn't care less about career paths. It's not important any more. When you want a baby, Jo-jo, it takes over your whole life. Everywhere you look, you see babies. And you want one.' She sighed. 'When you get broody, it's almost a physical need and nothing—I mean *nothing*—else matters. Your priorities change, and all you can think of is babies. Could you cope with that, knowing you couldn't have one?'

'I've never had to face it, so I don't know,' Jodie said.

'You can't just duck the issue, Jo-jo. You'll have to face it some time, and it'll test your love to the limits.'

'Maybe.' Jodie closed her eyes. 'I just know that I don't want to spend the rest of my life without Sam. Even if this baby thing hits me the way you and Sam think it will, I can't possibly feel as bad as I do now.'

'Then tell him,' Ellen said.

'I've tried.'

'And since when do you give up on anything, Jodie Price?'

Jodie gave a watery smile. Hadn't she already told Sam that she'd given up on him?

'Tell him, Jo-jo. Tell him how you feel. Tomorrow.'

But Jodie couldn't work up the nerve. Instead, she hid herself in paperwork, writing up case files. At least there was some good news—Ellie Langton's condition was back under control and Poppy Richardson was back home with her family, still coughing but well on the mend. Caitlin Truman's file was on Sam's list now; maybe she could patch things up with Julianne and ask to be kept updated.

She managed to avoid Sam for three days. He was busy with clinics and she volunteered for extra sessions in the paediatric assessment unit, so she didn't have to see him.

Though she pulled herself together and tried as much as possible to be her usual self on the ward, she found it incredibly difficult the day Sam did a teaching round. She

and Stuart and Duncan, the three junior doctors in the
ward, stood by the bed of Conor Bentley, a six-year-old
admitted with suspected myocarditis, inflammation of the
heart muscle, the previous day. He was asleep, his long
lashes shuttering the stunning navy-blue eyes all the
nurses on the ward had admired. Conor's sweet temper-
ament had endeared him to all, but his condition was so
serious that he might not pull through.

'OK, let's see what you know,' Sam said. 'Stuart—
what are the causes of myocarditis?'

'Bacterial, viral, parasitic and fungal,' he said swiftly.
'The inflammation can also be caused by rheumatic fever,
toxins, drugs and hypersensitive immune reactions.'

'Good. It can also be caused by surgery on the heart,
some medications and radiation therapy localised in the
chest,' Sam added. 'Out of the ones you mentioned,
which is rarest?'

'Parasitic—it's most often something like Chagas' disease.'

'Which is caused by?'

'An insect-borne protozoan, often in Central and South
America.'

Sam nodded. 'Most common?'

'Viral—which Conor has.'

'Good. Duncan, which viruses are implicated?'

'Coxsackie B—as in Conor's case, when he went
down with hand, foot and mouth disease at school. It can
also be caused by measles, the flu, chickenpox, the hep-
atitis virus or adenovirus,' the young doctor answered
confidently.

'Good—you've both been reading your stuff,' Sam
said, sounding pleased. 'Jodie. How is the diagnosis
made?'

'Through observation of symptoms, electrocardiogram

to record the heart's electrical activity, echo—' the ultra-
sound of the heart known as echocardiography '—which
will reveal an enlarged heart and poor contractions,
though in mild cases both the ECG and echo will appear
normal, angiography and endomyocardial biopsy.'

'And the biopsy is?'

'The removal of a piece of the endocardium, or the
lining membrane of the inner surface of the heart, usually
taken from around the right ventricle. It can determine
the cause as well as verify the disease, and helps us to
monitor potential congestive heart failure.'

'Good. You mentioned observation of symptoms.
Three each, please—Duncan, Stuart and Jodie.'

He'd gone in strict order, youngest and least experi-
enced first. It was only fair, but it felt as though Sam
were picking on her. And she also knew she only felt
like that because of the way he'd rejected her. From anyone else, she'd have taken it in her stride.

'Chest pain, rapid pulse, tiredness,' Duncan said.

'Feverishness, shortness of breath, swollen ankles,'
Stuart said.

'Palpitations, ventricular enlargement, pulmonary
oedema,' Jodie said.

'Good.' He paused. 'Stuart—prognosis?'

'If it's bacterial, it can be cured; if it's viral, it resolves
more slowly. Heart damage is a common result—and because that means the heart can't contract normally, heart
failure can develop.'

'And in this case,' Sam said softly, 'Conor has severe
arrhythmias. We may be talking about a transplant.'

'Do his parents know?' Duncan asked.

'They're coming in to see me tomorrow,' Sam said
heavily.

Jodie knew exactly what was coming next.

'Jodie, I'd like you to see the Bentleys with me.'

Why me? she asked silently. But she already knew: she was good with parents. Especially when it came to a case like this, where the child was so sick that a life-saving operation might be needed. 'Yes, Mr Taylor,' she said dully.

How could he be so dispassionate? Jodie had spent a lot of time sitting next to Conor's bed, playing with his dinosaurs and telling him how clever he was when he told her each of the names, syllable-perfect, what they ate and how they'd lived. It didn't seem fair that the life of a child could hang in the balance. There wouldn't be a dry eye on the ward if a transplant couldn't be ar-ranged—except possibly for Sam Taylor's.

And then, as they left Conor's bedside, ready to move on to the next case, Jodie caught a movement out of the corner of her eye. Sam was touching Conor's cheek with the backs of his fingers, a gesture of tenderness that brought a huge lump to her throat.

So he wasn't completely without emotion, then—just when it came to her. Which didn't make her feel any better. If anything, it made it worse to know that they'd shared something so special and yet it obviously hadn't meant the same to him. When she'd thought he'd said he loved her, it must have been some kind of auditory hal-lucination. Wishful thinking. Hearing what she so badly wanted to hear. Not the truth.

The next day, Jodie sat in Sam's office with Conor's parents.

'It's serious, Doctor, isn't it?' Mr Bentley asked.

Sam nodded. 'He's a very sick little boy. Unfortu-nately, the virus he picked up at school is known to cause heart problems in some cases, and Conor's been unlucky.

He may recover in time, but it'll be a limited recovery. If he forgets about his illness and exerts himself too much, his heart might stop working.'

'We've given him steroids to reduce the inflammation of his heart,' Jodie said, 'but there was a lot of damage. He's probably going to need a transplant.'

'You can't give him any other medication?' Mrs Bentley asked.

'I'm afraid not. Some cases can be treated with medication such as digitalis to stimulate a stronger heartbeat, but your son's heartbeat is extremely irregular. We feel a transplant will give him the best chance,' Sam said gently.

'How soon will it happen?' Mr Bentley asked.

'As soon as one becomes available. There has to be a tissue match, or Conor's body might reject the new heart,' Jodie said.

'We'll do anything,' Mr Bentley said. 'Anything. Conor's so precious to us. He's an IVF baby—we tried for years and years and thought it was too late for us. We'd saved up for one more cycle and said that would be the last one, and then we found we were expecting Conor.'

'Please. Don't let us lose our baby. Please. Please. Not now. Not like this,' Mrs Bentley begged, holding her husband's hand so tightly that her knuckles showed white.

Jodie met Sam's eyes and had to blink very hard. Would it be like that for them? Years and years and years of trying for the baby they both wanted so much—and then, when they at last had their precious baby, the risk of losing him…

No. She couldn't think of that right now. She had to concentrate on the Bentleys.

'We'll do our best, Mrs Bentley. He's a lovely little

boy.' She forced herself to smile, even though she felt like crying. 'And I think he knows more about dinosaurs than I ever will.'

'You should hear him about rockets. He's always saying he wants to be an astronaut.' Mr Bentley bit his lip. 'I don't suppose he will now.'

'Having a heart transplant doesn't mean he'll be an invalid for ever,' Jodie said quietly. 'And the surgeons at Papworth are amazing.'

'You won't do it here, then?' Mrs Bentley asked.

Jodie shook her head. 'He'll go to a specialist unit in Cambridge. I know the extra travelling time's going to be a bit of a pain for you—'

'Not where our boy's concerned,' Mr Bentley interrupted roughly. 'Even if he had to go to America—to Australia—we'd be with him every step of the way.'

'I know.' Jodie reached out to take his hand.

'What would a youngster like you know about it?' he asked nastily, pulling away from her. 'Got children of your own, have you?'

Jodie, realising how stressed and frustrated Conor's father must be feeling, didn't take it personally. He was only hitting out verbally at the nearest person, and if that helped him to cope with the situation, she could live with it. Even though he'd opened up wounds that had barely begun to heal. 'No, but I have a godson I adore, and I know how tough I'd find it if he were in Conor's place. And my baby sister died of a hole in the heart when I was younger, so I have a rough idea of how you must be feeling.'

'I'm sorry,' Mr Bentley said, shaking his head. 'I didn't mean to—'

'That's all right. No offence taken,' she cut in gently. 'And we'll do our best for Conor. I promise you that.'

'Thank you.'

'Look, can I get you a cup of tea? There's some paperwork to sort out with Mr Taylor, and I'm sure you could both do with some time to come to terms with it all,' she suggested gently.

'Thank you, love. That'd be nice,' Mrs Bentley said. Her voice was cracked with effort and Jodie guessed that she was trying not to cry.

Again, she inadvertently glanced at Sam. The look on his face was unreadable, but his eyes were definitely Wednesday morning grey. If she hadn't known better, she'd almost have thought he cared.

When Jodie had taken the Bentleys off for a cup of tea, Sam remained in his office, his head in his hands. He'd done the best for his patient's family, asking Jodie to talk to them, but it had been torture sitting there next to her. And then, when the Bentleys had talked about their IVF treatment—before then, he'd managed to avoid looking at Jodie. Just. But he hadn't been able to stop himself meeting her gaze.

A gaze that had said everything.

It could have been them—trying for years and years for an IVF baby. And even if it hadn't worked, they'd still have been together anyway, faced it as a team.

And he'd thrown it all away.

He groaned. She'd meet someone else. A warm, beautiful, bright and funny woman like Jodie—she'd soon find someone who deserved her. Someone who'd love her, someone who'd give her the child she wanted.

If only he could have been that someone.

CHAPTER ELEVEN

TIME for ward rounds, Jodie thought as she glanced at her watch. With any luck, Sam would be busy with a parent or at clinic, so she wouldn't have to face him.

But luck wasn't on her side. Yes, he was at clinic—but it finished at the same time as her ward round. Which meant that he opened the door to the ward and walked straight into her as she was leaving.

'Hello, Jodie,' he said.

'You look like hell.' The words were out before she could stop them.

The corner of his mouth twitched.

She closed her eyes. 'I— Look, I'm not brilliant at tact.'

'Uh-huh.'

At least he sounded amused rather than annoyed. She opened her eyes again. He really did look like hell. There were dark shadows under his eyes and his skin looked almost grey with fatigue and misery. As if he'd been suffering as much as she had, night after night of staring up at the ceiling at three a.m., wishing for what couldn't be. 'Are you OK?'

'I'll live,' he said dryly. 'You?'

To her horror, she found tears welling up. She rushed to the nearest loo and intended to bolt the door against him, but she wasn't fast enough.

'Jodie. Don't cry. Please, don't cry.' He followed her in, locked the door behind him and cradled her in his arms. 'I never wanted to hurt you.'

She simply sobbed against his shoulder.

'Oh, Jodie.' He stroked her hair, holding her close.

'I c-can't do this,' she hiccuped against his shoulder. 'I can't go through every day knowing you're going to leave and I'm never going to see you again.'

'I have to go, Jodie.'

'No, you don't. And I'm never going to feel less miserable than I do now if you leave.'

'You'll get over me.'

She raised a tear-stained face to meet his gaze. 'No, I won't. You're the one I want. I love you, Sam, and I think you love me.'

'Jodie—'

'You said it. In your office. When we…' She swallowed. 'I heard you. I'm sure I heard you. Unless that was just—' her voice wobbled '—wishful thinking?'

He was silent.

So he wasn't denying it. Her heart lifted. Maybe it was going to work out after all. 'I need you, Sam. I want you. I love you. And I don't care about this baby thing.'

'You will.'

'How do you know? You can't predict the future.'

'Neither can you,' he pointed out. 'It's for the best. Trust me—'

'You're a doctor,' she finished bitterly. 'Sam, it's tearing me apart. I can't sleep, I can't eat, I can't think straight. And you look just as bad.'

'I feel it,' he muttered.

'We need to talk.' She scrubbed at her eyes with the back of her hand. 'Not here.'

'Neutral ground,' he said.

'Somewhere quiet, where we're not going to be disturbed.' She swallowed. 'My place, at seven. I'll cook.'

'Jodie—'

'We need to talk. Please, Sam,' she said.

He nodded. 'All right. Your place at seven.'

He wiped away a tear with his thumb, and the intimate gesture almost made her cry again. But she managed to go back to the ward, write up her notes and then head for the supermarket.

I'll cook. Ha. Why had she said that, when she knew she burned everything? For a moment she was tempted to ring Ellen in a panic and ask for help. But then she pulled herself together. The food wasn't that important—the talking bit was far more crucial. And even *I* can bung chicken breasts in the oven, heat up a sachet of sauce and microwave a bag of mixed vegetables, Jodie thought as she stared at the supermarket shelves. Followed by some out-of-season strawberries and luxury praline ice cream, and there was probably something in the wine rack at home that would go with it.

By the time she'd cycled home, had a shower and changed, laid the dining-room table and sorted out what needed to go where and when in the kitchen, it was nearly seven and the doorbell rang.

Sam leaned on the doorjamb, holding a carrier bag and a large bunch of pale delicate orchids.

'Thank you,' she said quietly, accepting them.

'I forgot to ask you if you preferred red or white. So I bought both,' he said, gesturing to the carrier bag.

'Thanks.' She nodded. 'Come in.'

She arranged the flowers in a blue glass jug and put them on the kitchen window-sill. Sam had brought her flowers. Goodbye or hello flowers? she wondered. Her throat tightened and she dug her nails into the palms of her hands to stop herself crying. They were going to discuss this calmly and rationally, like adults—which meant she wasn't going to give in to her feelings and fling herself in his arms and howl her eyes out.

'Wine?' she asked, taking glasses from a cupboard.

'I'm driving,' he reminded her.

'One glass?'

'With dinner.'

Lord, this was impossible. This was the man she loved, the man she was sure loved her—and yet here they were, acting like polite strangers.

'Have a seat. Dinner will be—' she checked the microwave clock '—three minutes.'

'Anything I can do to help?'

Lots. But not in the way he meant. 'It's fine,' she said.

The three minutes felt more like three hours, but at last the vegetables were ready. Jodie dished up the chicken, poured the sauce over it and added the vegetables, tiny new potatoes and runner beans and broccoli florets and carrot sticks. Sam took the plates and followed her into the dining room, where she lit a candle in the middle of the table.

'White OK with you?' she asked, waving the bottle and the corkscrew at him. Being Sam, he'd brought the white wine already chilled.

'Fine.'

One glass, she remembered.

'D'you want me to…?' He indicated the bottle.

'No, it's OK.' She deftly uncorked the bottle and poured them both a glass.

He took a mouthful of chicken. 'This is good.'

'Chiller cabinet,' she confessed. 'I'm…er, cooking's not really my thing.'

There was nothing he could say to that.

They both resorted to concentrating on their food and avoiding the subject they both knew they had to discuss, and the silence grew worse and worse. Why on earth had she suggested this? Instead of making things better, she'd made it a million times worse. The candle had been a mistake, too. The light softened the hard lines of his face and made him look…delectable. That was the only word for it. How was she going to talk rationally to him, argue her case, when her libido sprang into action and turned her mind into soup just because of the way he looked? And if she started thinking about the way his body felt against hers… Bad idea.

She gulped down a glass of the excellent Chablis without even tasting it and poured herself another—then looked up to see the corner of Sam's mouth quirking.

'What?'

'Since when have you needed alcohol to loosen your tongue?'

She flushed. He had a point. And he'd barely touched his own glass. 'All right. Since you brought up the subject, it's time we talked.'

He sat back and folded his arms. 'It was a very nice meal. Thanks.'

She ignored the obvious diversion tactics. 'I asked you here to talk about us. And we do need to discuss it—it's not going to go away. Sam, I can't stand being without you.'

'Yes, you can. I'm leaving soon, and you'll be fine.'

'I won't. And I don't understand how someone so clever can be so—so—so *stupid*!' she burst out.

'Stupid?' His brow furrowed.

'Can't you see what's right under your nose? Sam, you're miserable and I'm miserable. Why can't we be miserable together?'

'Now, there's an offer,' he said dryly.

'Don't joke. Not about this.'

'No.' He paused. 'Let's go for the million-pound question, then. Do you want a baby—and I don't mean right now, I mean at some point in the future?'

Jodie lifted her chin. She'd been asking herself that question for days. Now was the time to be honest. 'Yes. Yes, I do.'

'So that rules me out as your partner.'

'No, it damn well doesn't!' She banged the table and then rubbed her sore hand, angry with herself for reacting so childishly. So much for discussing things rationally, in an adult way. She took a deep breath and began again. 'Sam, just because you have infertility problems, it doesn't mean we can't ever have a baby. There are lots of things we could do. I've been looking into it.'

'Oh, have you?' he asked, his voice dangerously soft.

She refused to be intimidated. 'Yes. I did a search on Medline.' She noted the sudden set look to his jaw. 'Here, before you say it, not at work. And I haven't said a word to anyone else about it.'

He gave her a look as if he didn't quite believe her—they both knew she was quite capable of buttonholing a consultant from Obs and Gynae and asking them about a 'friend's' case.

Maybe she should try a different tack. 'Sam, if you—if you didn't have this problem, if you'd met me and we'd done all the things that normal couples do, maybe even got married and tried to start a family, and then we'd found out I was the one who couldn't have children…would you have walked out on me?'

He just looked at her.

'Would you?' she persisted.

For a moment, she didn't think he was going to answer. Then, finally, his shoulders sagged slightly. 'No.'

'You wouldn't have deserted me,' she said, as if to

confirm his words. 'So why do you expect me to abandon you, just because the position's reversed?'

He shrugged. 'Experience.'

'Angela?'

He closed his eyes. 'Yes.'

She reached across the table and took his hand. 'Sam. Talk to me. Tell me what happened. It's not because I want all the sordid details—'

'I know,' he cut in, looking embarrassed, as if remembering the last time he'd flung that accusation at her.

'Maybe it'd do you good to tell someone,' she said softly, 'instead of keeping all the hurt locked inside.'

Was he going to answer her? Or was he going to refuse to discuss it and walk straight out of the door? For what seemed like hours she really wasn't sure. And then, finally, his fingers tightened around hers.

'I met Angela at university.' His voice was so quiet, she could hardly hear him. 'She was reading law and she was heading for the top—nothing would stand in the way of her career.' His smile held a tinge of bitterness. 'You remind me of her, in the early days—full of life, so sure of where you're going and yet with a sense of fun to stop you being too serious. I'd decided to specialise in oncology, and I was working for my exams. I thought we were happy together.'

And now he'd started talking, it was, oh, so easy to tell Jodie—to explain how the bottom had dropped out of his world and how he couldn't face it happening again.

'And then one day she said she wanted a baby.' His jaw clenched. 'We tried for nearly eighteen months. Eighteen months of using ovulation kits, only making love on the right days, being careful what we did and ate and drank. Eighteen months of her crying every time her period started, asking why we couldn't make a baby when all her friends were falling the first time they tried. Especially when we were only in our mid-twenties, at the peak of our fertility.

'That's when we went for tests and we found out I couldn't have children. She still wanted a baby, more than anything else in the world—so she left me for someone who could give her what she wanted.' His face twisted. 'My failure wrecked more than just two lives, Jodie. She left me for her boss. He was married with children, but I suppose that was part of the attraction. If I'd been the husband she wanted, her boss's family would still have been together now.'

'You don't know that. Maybe…maybe they would have fallen in love with each other anyway,' Jodie suggested.

'Maybe. Maybe not.' He sighed. 'But I'm at least partly to blame. If I'd given her what she needed, she wouldn't have had to look elsewhere.'

'Sam, sometimes you think you're in love with someone, and then you meet someone else and realise…' Her voice faded. She'd thought she'd loved Graham, and she'd been hurt and angry and upset when he'd left her. And yet what had happened between Sam and her on Christmas Day had shown her she hadn't even begun to know what love was. What she had with Sam was something else. Something special. Something she didn't want to lose.

He disentangled his hand from hers, restoring the distance between them. 'So now you know the whole sorry mess.'

She nodded, guessing what was worrying him. 'I'll respect your confidence.'

'Thank you.'

His eyes were definitely Wednesday morning grey

again, and there were finely etched lines of strain around them, Jodie thought. Maybe he was remembering the way Angela had broken his heart, the despair he'd felt when she'd left.

'Sam, I'm not Angela,' she reminded him. 'I'm a completely different person. I want different things out of life.'

'You want a baby,' he said doggedly.

'Eventually, yes.' She looked at him. 'Don't you?'

He flinched. 'Why ask me when you know I can't?'

'What I'm trying to say, Sam, is that it's not just your problem. It's *ours*. So we'll face it together, as a couple. We'll support each other through it and we'll solve it. There are all sorts of things we could do. There's ICSI, for a start.' ICSI, or intra-cytoplasmic sperm injection, was a specialised form of IVF which helped in cases of low sperm count. A single sperm was picked up in a very fine glass needle and injected directly into the egg cell, and the fertilised embryos were then returned to the womb. Jodie had seen figures putting the success rate of the treatment at around twenty-five per cent, which was almost as good as the chances of the average couple conceiving naturally with unprotected sex.

She knew it would be gruelling for both of them—she'd need to take drugs to increase the number of eggs her ovaries released, for the length of the treatment cycle—but it would be worth it to see Sam holding his child in his arms. A little boy with those same beautiful grey eyes and dark hair and beautiful mouth.

'There are all sorts of options,' she repeated. 'All we need to do is talk to a specialist.'

Sam folded his arms. How many specialists had he seen with Angela? His GP, the fertility clinic, the endless tests, the indignity of giving samples...and all for noth-

ing. For one lousy piece of paper that condemned him as
forever childless. Sure, medicine advanced quickly—
everyone knew that—but it hadn't advanced far enough
to help him. And he couldn't face going through it all
again, seeing the hope blossom every time in Jodie's face
as they started treatment and then die again as yet another
cycle passed with no success. And then seeing that hope
turn to resentment, dislike, even hate…

Jodie recognised the set look on his face. Mr Frosty
again. Was she ever going to thaw him out? She took a
deep breath. 'You want a baby—so do I. You want me
and I want you. We want the same thing, Sam. So what's
the problem?'

'You know what the problem is.' He spoke quietly,
normally, and that made it a hundred times worse. If he'd
shouted, been hurt and angry, at least he'd have been
feeling something, she thought. As it was, he just
sounded…hopeless.

'Sperm.'

'What?'

'That's the problem. Sperm.' A tiny little thing that
you couldn't even see without a microscope—and it
stood between them like a mountain. If it wasn't so tragic
she would have laughed at the incongruity. As it was,
she was having a hard time stopping herself crying. 'Your
turn for the million-dollar question. Do you love me,
Sam?'

He swallowed hard. 'Jodie, that isn't fair.'

'It's as fair as your question,' she retorted. 'Do you
love me?'

'No.'

'Liar.'

He closed his eyes. 'Jodie…'

'Or maybe you're right,' she said. 'If you loved me,

you wouldn't put me through the wringer like this. You'd give us a chance. Sure, it might not work out between us. It might not work out for a million and one reasons. You might find you can't stand having a partner who can't cook and never tidies up and leaves wet towels on the bathroom floor. I might change my mind and decide I don't want a baby at some point in the future, that I want to be a hotshot consultant in one of the top jobs in the country. I might not even be able to have children. I don't know. But is it really worth throwing everything away for the sake of something that *might* happen in the future?'

'God, help me, Jodie, I do love you,' he said, his voice hoarse. 'And that's why I have to go, why I have to stay away from you. I don't want to see you torn apart the way Angela was.'

Why did everything always have to come back to Angela? If Jodie ever met the wretched woman, she'd want to strangle her for the damage she'd caused to Sam. Could that damage ever be repaired? Could her own love for Sam heal his wounds? More to the point, would he even let her try? She sighed. 'We're back to stalemate again, aren't we?'

'Jodie, I don't want to break your heart.'

'You're doing that already.'

'I'm sorry. I…' He stood up. 'I'd better go.'

'So you're just going to walk out on me, without even discussing it?'

'We *have* discussed it.'

'Hardly.' She walked round the table and placed her hand on his arm. 'Sam, I just don't understand why you won't give us a chance.'

He sighed. 'Because this infertility thing's too big. I've

already wrecked enough lives over it. I don't want to ruin yours as well.'

'It'd be ruined without you,' she said simply.

'We're going round in circles, Jodie, and it isn't helping either of us.'

Her eyes pricked with tears and she tried to blink them back. 'Please, Sam…' His name came out as a wobble.

'I have to go. For both our sakes.'

But it was already too late. The touch of her skin against his was enough to send him up in flames. Unable to help himself, he reached out and tugged her into his arms. The next thing he knew, he was kissing her with a starving desperation matched by her own.

He pulled himself away from her with an effort. 'We shouldn't be doing this,' he warned.

She said nothing, but the look on her face reminded him of the first time he'd made love to her, in the light of the Christmas tree, when she'd looked like an angel. Even with reddened eyes and a face flushed by misery and anger, she was still beautiful. And he wanted her more than ever before. With a muffled curse at his foolishness, his inability to resist her when he knew he ought to give her up, he swung her up into his arms and carried her up the stairs. His feet found the way to her room as if he'd been there a million times, instead of just the once.

Afterwards, he wasn't sure who had undressed who—there was a trail of clothes on the floor that suggested they'd started at the doorway—but, lying there with her in his arms, her head pillowed against his chest and the soft honey scent of her skin and hair in his nose, he felt as if he'd come home.

At least, his heart told him he was home—but his mind told him it wasn't permanent. He didn't want a short, passionate fling. He wanted Jodie for keeps. But it wasn't possible. Whatever she said, he was sure it would be the same with her as it had been with Angela. A beginning full of hope, a hope that slowly seeped away and took their love with it.

Which meant he had to leave. Now.

But she obviously felt him beginning to withdraw, because she tangled her legs between his. 'Sam. Don't go,' she said softly.

'I have to. The cat.' It was an excuse, even though it was partly true.

And she obviously knew it. 'Do you have a cat-flap?' she asked.

'Yes.'

'And neighbours who'll give her a snack if she turns up at their door?'

He laughed softly. 'She's a dab hand at getting what she wants.' Just like Jodie, he thought wryly. She wanted him—and he knew full well he ought to leave now *now*, before both of them got hurt even more. 'Yes.'

'Then she'll be fine tonight,' she said. 'She won't starve and she can go in and out as she pleases. Stay with me tonight, Sam. Go home in the morning.'

His head warned him not to listen, to go now, but his heart made him reach out to stroke her hair, and his mouth refused to form the words it was supposed to say. 'Are you on duty tomorrow?'

'Day off. You?'

Early, his head said. *Tell her early.*

His mouth rebelled again. 'Late.'

'Hmm.'

That sultry note in Jodie's voice made his defences crumble even more. 'There's a very wanton look on your face, Dr Price.'

'Is there, now?' It wasn't really a question. She slid her hand over his chest, her fingers tangling in the dark curls and then moving purposefully lower.

Sam gasped. 'Keep that up and I'll—'

She smiled. 'That's the idea.'

'I can't think straight when you touch me.'

Her smile broadened. 'Good. Maybe you'll start thinking with your heart instead of your head.'

'Jo—'

She cut him off by the simple expedient of kissing him, and he stopped thinking altogether.

CHAPTER TWELVE

THE next morning, Sam woke with Jodie in his arms. It was still early but enough light filtered through her cream bedroom curtains to let him see her face. He watched her sleep, thinking how soft and kissable her mouth looked. And then she moved slightly, murmuring something that sounded suspiciously like his name.

Was she dreaming of him? he wondered. And the way she was smiling in her sleep... It must be some dream, he thought with a grin, to put that kind of look on her face. He couldn't resist bending to kiss the tip of her nose.

She woke immediately and blinked hard, as if adjusting to her surroundings and trying to remember what had happened the previous night. Then her smile broadened. 'Sam.'

'Good morning.'

She reached up to touch his face. 'Mmm. Do I get a proper good morning?'

He laughed, and kissed her. 'Like this, you mean?' he teased.

'You're getting there.' She kissed him back, and Sam's heartbeat accelerated.

Before his mind had a chance to step in and remind him he wasn't supposed to be doing this, he was supposed to be finding a way to let her down gently and bow out of her life, his fingers were stroking her skin, pleasuring them both as she arched up against his touch.

'That'll do nicely, Mr Taylor,' she breathed as he bent to suckle a nipple. 'Very nicely indeed...'

Sam, in turn, sighed with pleasure as he sank into her. She felt so good, so right—as if this was what he'd been meant to do all his life. And although his head was frantically trying to tell him to stop right now and be sensible about things, his body wasn't listening. At all.

They lay curled together in silence afterwards, with Sam's arms wrapped tightly round her. He wanted to stay like this for ever, but he had commitments. That hadn't changed. 'I'd better get up.' He kissed her protests away and gently disentangled himself from her arms.

Jodie snuggled back against the pillows, watching him dress. 'It's only seven o'clock,' she informed him after a glance at her alarm clock. 'Can't you stay a bit longer? Just a *tiny* bit?'

Lord, it was tempting. Sam wanted to crawl back into her bed and never, ever leave it. He shook himself. 'I really do have to go. I'd better check on Sooty. The cat,' he added at her faintly puzzled look. He bent down to kiss her again. 'But I'll be back later.'

'Promise?'

Her eyes were very green. Fear? Worried that his head would take over from his heart again and he'd go frosty on her? He might try, but he'd learned during the night that Jodie Price wouldn't give up until she had what she wanted.

And what Jodie wanted, hard as it was to believe, was *him*.

He smiled. 'Promise.'

Jodie smiled back. Everything was going to be all right, she thought with a leap of joy. He'd finally, finally come round to her way of thinking. The night they'd just spent together proved that. And the future was starting to look distinctly rosy.

But by lunchtime Jodie realised he wasn't coming back. Maybe there'd been an emergency on the ward and he hadn't had a chance to call her first, she thought. He'd probably ring her later. Maybe he'd even come straight round after his shift.

When nine o'clock that evening came and went, she had to face it. Sam wasn't coming back at all. His promise had been like pie-crust—full of air and easily broken.

Unable to bear spending the night in sheets that still smelled of him, she changed the duvet. Then, realising it still wasn't enough—there were too many memories and her double bed suddenly seemed way too big—she made up the bed in her spare room and tried to sleep there.

It didn't work.

She just spent the night awake, wishing she knew what had gone wrong and what exactly was going on in Sam's head.

The following morning, she was on early shift, and she lasted until nearly lunchtime before she walked into Julianne's office.

'Can I help you?' Julianne asked, with her best ask-me-if-you-dare face on.

'I, um, wondered if I could have a word with Sam. About the Bentleys.'

Julianne gave her what Jodie could only describe as a pitying look. 'Haven't you heard? Mr Taylor's away.'

Away? Since when? 'When's he due back?' Jodie asked carefully.

Julianne shrugged. 'No idea.'

'I didn't think he was on holiday.'

Julianne shrugged again.

Jodie gritted her teeth. When she made it to consultant level, she'd insist on having a secretary who didn't abuse her power and make everyone else's life a misery. Someone who realised that other people had a job to do, too. 'So what are the rest of us supposed to do in the meantime?'

'Richard's taking over his cases.'

'Right.' She had to know what was going on. But how could she find out without Julianne suspecting something and spreading rumours? She forced a smile to her face and said casually, 'A bit sudden, isn't it?'

'What?'

'Going away without a word to his firm. Must be difficult for you. Juggling the diary is tough at the best of times.'

Julianne clearly wasn't falling for that one. 'He told *some* of us,' she said loftily.

Sam had been *planning* to go away? He'd known before he'd spent the night with her? He'd promised her he'd be back later—and yet he'd still left. Jodie searched through her memory. He'd said he'd applied for another job, but he hadn't said *when* he was leaving.

And Julianne hadn't said he was going away for ever.

Sam himself had said he'd be back. He'd *promised*. 'Patient?' Jodie asked, hoping Julianne hadn't noticed the slight quiver in her voice.

'Personal reasons,' the secretary said loftily. 'I'm afraid I can't discuss them.'

Personal reasons. Meaning me? Jodie thought wretchedly. He's walked out on me again without a word. This time for good. So much for promises.

'OK. I'll talk to Richard later,' she said, doing her best to appear insouciant. And all the while her heart was ripping into tiny, unmendable shreds.

*   *   *

'Sam.' Mary Taylor looked at her son and squeezed his hand, her grey eyes softening. She pulled the oxygen mask from her face. 'My boy,' she gasped.

He stroked her cheek. 'Can I get you anything, Mum? Water?'

She shook her head, the movement clearly an effort. 'Need to talk,' she murmured wheezily.

'No, Mum.' Her sentences were fractured, each word requiring enormous effort, and Sam didn't want her taxing her strength. 'Don't strain yourself. I'm not going anywhere.'

'My fault.'

'Nothing's your fault, Mum,' he reassured her. 'It's pneumonia. Anyone could have got it. And you're in the best hands. You're going to be fine.'

'No. You and Angela. It's all my fault. I should have gone to the doctor's when you were little,' she whispered brokenly.

Sam flinched. 'It's all in the past. You weren't to know. Don't blame yourself, Mum.'

'Have to talk.'

Sam frowned and was about to ask her what she meant, but she drifted back to sleep. He replaced the oxygen mask over her face and sat back in the chair beside her bed, holding her hand and keeping half an eye on the monitor beside her, watching the numbers change in line with his mother's breathing and pulse. Funny to think that just over twelve hours ago he'd been holding a woman's hand in bed. Except it had been his lover's, not his mother's.

He closed his eyes. He really had to ring Jodie. She must have thought he'd run out on her—but when his mobile had rung and the hospital in Cornwall had told him his mother had been admitted with pneumonia and was asking for him, his immediate reaction had been to drop off his key at his neighbour's and ask her to feed the cat, then drive straight up to be at his mother's sickbed. He'd known his mother had had a flu-like illness a week or so before, but she'd assured him that the warden of the sheltered flats where she lived was keeping an eye on her and she was fine. He knew, however, that bacterial pneumonia could come on suddenly, as it had in his mother's case. Gently, he released his mother's hand and checked her notes again. Respirations rapid and laboured, chest radiograph demonstrating consolidation in the right lower lobe, sputum analysis showing positive Gram stain for bacterial pneumococci, increased white blood cell count.

Which was why Mary was sitting up in bed—to help her lung expansion—plus she was on twenty-four per cent oxygen through a mask and six-hourly antibiotics. She'd be in hospital for a good seven days, he thought. Seven days when he really needed to be here for his mother, plus a couple of days to make sure she'd settled back at home and could manage on her own again, with help from the carers at the complex.

Which made it ten days until he could be with Jodie again.

He'd tried ringing her a couple of times on the way to Cornwall, when he'd taken a break from the eight-hour drive, but she hadn't answered. She hadn't answered during the afternoon either. Maybe she'd gone out somewhere—it was her day off after all. If she had an answering machine, it wasn't switched on. He only hoped she'd tried ringing him on the ward and they'd told her he'd phoned in and said he'd be away for a few days.

'Mum, I won't be long. I just need to call Jodie,' he told the sleeping woman.

He told the nurse on the desk where he was going, then headed over to the payphone by the visitors' room. A woman with red-rimmed eyes was talking brokenly into the receiver. Not wanting to disturb her by asking how long she'd be, Sam decided to go outside and use his mobile.

The phone rang for three minutes, then a polite voice informed him, 'There is no reply.' And cut him off.

He glanced at his watch. Obviously Jodie was still out. He'd try again later.

Mary's eyes were still closed when he returned to her room, and her breathing was still laboured.

'I've made such a mess of things, Mum,' he told his sleeping parent. 'I've met someone—someone really special. She's a doctor, too. You'd adore her. Her name's Jodie, and she's the most beautiful woman I've ever met. She hardly ever wears a scrap of make-up, her hair goes wild in the rain, she rides this dreadful old boneshaker that her big brother handed down to her years back, and she's got the eyes of an angel.'

He sighed. 'She tried to get me out of my shell. Would you believe, she fed me avocado on pizza? She's got this crazy streak. She's untidy. She's nearly always late. She never wears a white coat when she's supposed to. She drinks frothy coffee but she doesn't like chocolate on the top. She hates dried fruit but she'd live on chocolate if she could. The patients love her, their parents love her, everyone on the ward loves her, and I want her more than anything in the world…but she wants babies. Babies I can't give her. And I don't know where we go from here. She thinks we can get through this together, but I'm not so sure. I want a baby with her, but it just isn't going to happen. Not with me as the biological father, anyway. I've got to accept that. I know there are people much, much worse off than I am, and you can't always have what you want.' He sighed. 'Maybe she's right, maybe there is someone who can help us have a baby. Or maybe not. I don't know.'

He stroked the back of Mary's hand with his thumb. 'I'm no good at talking things through. Patients and their families, yes—I can do that, tell them all the options and help them come to a decision. But when it comes to my own life…I've never been any good at it. Even as a child. I don't know how to do it. I just freeze up and the words I really want to say won't come out. That was half the trouble with Angela. If we'd talked, *really* talked, maybe we could have saved our marriage.' He smiled ruefully. 'I guess you and Dad were like that, too. You never talked—at least, not when I was around. I never told him how much I loved him before he died.' He bit his lip. 'I don't remember him ever telling me he loved me either. But that was Dad. I'm—well, I'm going to try to be different. When you wake up again, I'm going to tell you. I'm going to talk to you about everything. And maybe you can help me find the right words to say to Jodie. Tell her how I really feel.'

He swallowed hard. 'But maybe it's too late for that.'

The minutes ticked by. When it reached half past nine and Mary was still asleep, Sam bent over to kiss her cheek. 'I'm going to try Jodie again now, Mum. I'll be back in a minute.'

This time, the payphone was free. Sam dialled Jodie's number and willed her to answer…but there was no reply. So either she still wasn't back—or she'd given up on him and gone to see Ellen. 'When this is all over, Jodie Price, I swear I'm going to buy you an answering

machine and make you use it,' he said through gritted
teeth. If he couldn't get hold of her later, he'd have to
ring her on the ward and to hell with the grapevine.

Mary was awake again when he returned to her room.

'Sam.' She smiled weakly and removed the mask.

'Mum, put it back. You need it,' he warned.

She ignored him. 'Did you have something to eat?'

He shook his head. 'I went to make a phone call.'

'You have to eat properly.'

He grinned. 'Mum, I'm a doctor. I'm hardly likely to
starve myself.' He sat back down by her bed. 'How do
you feel?'

'Silly,' she said. 'All this fuss.'

'You're worth it.' He squeezed her hand. 'I want you
to get well again. You need to rest.'

'We need to talk,' she said again. 'What happened—
you and Angela.'

'It's all in the past, Mum. Please, don't upset yourself.
Wait until you're feeling better. We'll discuss it later. Put
the mask back on.'

'No. We have to talk now.' She looked hard at him.
'About babies.'

He swallowed hard. 'They're not an option for me,
Mum. I'm sorry. And Angela and I—'

'Not Angela. Jodie.'

His eyes widened. 'Jodie?'

'The one who looks like an angel.'

Sam stared at her in shock. Had she heard everything
he'd said when he'd been burbling on? 'You mean…you
were listening? I thought you were asleep.'

Mary shook her head slowly. 'Just resting my eyes.'

He nodded soberly. 'I guess you know everything,
then.'

A tear trickled down her face. 'No good at talking—that's my fault. I never showed you how.'

'It doesn't matter now.' He squeezed her hand. 'I love you, Mum.'

'I love you, Sam.' Her eyes glittered. 'I never told you enough.'

Just as he was about to protest, he remembered how distant his parents had both seemed during his child-hood—not like his friends' parents, never wanting to play games or rough-and-tumble. There had been no sponta-neous hugs, no embarrassing but affectionate nicknames. He'd just assumed it had been because they were older, from another generation. Or maybe he hadn't been planned and his parents hadn't really known how to re-spond to him.

It was a sobering thought.

'Does she love you?' Mary asked suddenly.

'Jodie?' He nodded. 'She says so.'

'Then she'll understand about the babies.' Mary squeezed his fingers. 'Talk to her. Follow your heart. It's not too late.'

Maybe. But if he didn't manage to talk to her soon, it would be. Much, much too late.

Jodie didn't answer her phone even at eleven o'clock that night. OK, stop panicking, Sam told himself. She's prob-ably spending the night at Ellen's. Though he couldn't ring her there because he didn't know Ellen's surname, let alone her phone number—there was no way he could find out either. I'll ring again in the morning, he decided.

He did. Still there was no answer.

Which meant he had no other choice. He'd have to ring the ward. He didn't know what shift she was on, but if he rang at two he had a good chance of catching her, whether she was on early or late.

Two o'clock. How was he going to get through the hours until then?

'Explain,' Mary whispered later that morning.

'Explain what?'

'Babies. Why they're not an option.'

He flushed. Talking about something so deeply personal would be hard enough, but to discuss it with his mother, when they'd never really talked about things... Though he'd done it earlier, when he'd thought she'd been asleep. What was so different now? 'Angela and I tried for a long while with no luck. We both had tests and they said I couldn't have children.'

'What about a test-tube baby?'

IVF, in common parlance. He shook his head. 'The problem was with me, not her, so it wouldn't have worked.'

She flinched. 'If I'd taken you to see th—'

'It probably wouldn't have made any difference,' Sam cut in firmly. That wasn't strictly true, but he didn't want his mother worrying about it and setting back her progress. Right now, her own health was more important.

'But they can do more things now, can't they?' she asked hopefully.

'There's AID—artificial insemination by donor,' he said heavily. 'Or adoption.'

She nodded. 'Go home. Tell her how you feel.'

'I am *not* leaving you on your own in hospital, Mum.'

'Go home,' Mary repeated.

Sam folded his arms. His mother might have a stubborn streak, but he'd inherited it. In spades. 'Not a chance. I'm staying put until I'm satisfied you're better.'

Mary sighed. 'Then ring her. Now.'

But when he got through to the ward, Jodie was on her rounds and couldn't be interrupted. Sam almost said, 'Even for an emergency?' But it wasn't exactly that.

Or was it?

In the end, he said, 'No message. I'll try again later.'

The next time he rang, Jodie was on her break and had apparently gone for a walk.

The next, she was with parents and couldn't be disturbed.

Sam gritted his teeth and dialled a familiar number.

'Dr Taylor's secretary,' a brisk voice informed him.

'Julianne, it's Sam. I, um, need a favour.'

'Oh?' Her voice switched from cool and professional to fluttery—or was it just his imagination? Lack of sleep and too much worry, he told himself. Julianne saw him as another white coat, nothing else.

'I need to talk to Dr Price about something and I can't get hold of her.'

'Maybe one of the other doctors can help?'

'No. No, it's—' Sam stopped himself before he said *personal*. 'It's a case she's been dealing with, so she's the one with all the information.' It wasn't an outright lie. He just hadn't said *who* the case was. Himself. 'Could you ask her to ring me when she gets a moment?' He gave her the reception number for his mother's ward. 'Tell her to ask for me.'

'Of course, Sam. Whenever I see her next.'

'Thanks, Julianne.'

'Do you know when you'll be back?'

'Not yet. As soon as I can.' He sighed. 'I'll try to ring in again tomorrow. If anyone needs me urgently, give them this number—but I do mean urgent.'

'Of course. I'll make sure no one disturbs you unnec-essarily.'

Sam was smiling when he replaced the receiver. He was aware that the junior doctors called his secretary 'the dragon'—and probably something even more uncompli-mentary in private. If he hadn't been her boss, he'd prob-ably be terrified of her himself, he thought wryly. But at least he knew she was efficient. He could trust her to pass on the message. Then Jodie would ring him, he could explain—and, please, God, there'd be a happy-ever-after.

Jodie walked along the corridor to Julianne's office. At the door, she paused, turned on her heel and walked briskly back the other way. There was no point in beard-ing Sam's secretary in her den. If Julianne did know any more, she wouldn't be telling. For some reason, Julianne seemed to dislike Jodie even more than she did the other junior doctors and was particularly intractable with her.

No, she was going to do the sensible thing. She went to Richard's office instead.

The head of Paediatrics was elbow-deep in paperwork when she knocked on his door. 'Hello, Jodie.' He smiled warmly at her. 'What can I do for you?'

'It's appalling timing, I know, but I need a favour.' She bit her lip. 'I need to take a few days off.'

'Problems at home?' he guessed.

'Sort of.' She sighed. 'Right now, I'm a liability to the others. I'm not thinking straight and I don't want to put a patient at risk.'

He frowned. 'Jodie, this isn't like you. Is there any-thing I can do to help?'

She shook her head, her eyes pricking with tears. Trust Richard to be kind. But there was nothing anyone could do to help. Not any more. Sam wouldn't let anyone close enough. 'I—I just need a bit of time to sort my head out. A couple of days?'

'Take the rest of the week,' Richard said. 'Go home to your parents. It looks as if you could do with some spoiling, young lady.'

'But with—' she just managed to stop herself saying 'Sam' '—Mr Taylor being away—'

'We'll just have to crack the whip a bit and make Duncan and Stuart work harder,' he told her with a wink that told her he'd do the extra hours himself—Richard never had run the department by imperious demands. 'Lyn offered to do a few more hours if we needed more cover. I'll ask her if she can step into the breach for you. And if she can't there are a couple of others I can try.'

'Thanks, Richard.' She smiled wanly at him. 'I'm sorry, I just...'

'It's OK. Everyone hits a rough patch at some time. We'll all muck in until everything's sorted. Don't worry about it—take your time and come back when you're ready. And if you need to talk about anything, you know I'm here.'

'Thanks.' The lump in her throat prevented her saying any more.

Two days later, Sam realised that Jodie wasn't going to ring him. A day's wait he'd be able to reason round— maybe Julianne hadn't had a chance to see her, Jodie was rushed off her feet on the ward, or she'd been working late and fallen asleep as soon as she got home.

But two days?

Give her the benefit of the doubt, the voice in his head urged. *Ring Julianne. Ask her.*

He did.

'I'm sorry, Sam, I'm afraid I haven't seen her,' Julianne said crisply. 'I think she's away for a few days.'

Since when?

Sam closed his eyes, hoping he hadn't made that last comment out loud. 'Thanks anyway.' He rang off and stared at the receiver. He wasn't aware of any conferences Jodie would have been attending, and he knew he hadn't signed anything to send her on developmental training. And surely she'd have said she had a week off, not just a day, when he'd asked her about her shift that morning?

That morning, which seemed so very long ago now, when he'd woken with her in his arms...

Or maybe she'd changed her duty since then. Since she thought he'd run out on her. And because he'd been so determined to talk to her, tell her how he felt, he'd lost his chance. If only he'd written her a letter, sent her flowers at work—anything rather than leave cryptic messages via his secretary.

Yet he couldn't have told Julianne what it was all about. Jodie needed to hear it from him, not someone else.

Hell, what a mess. How was he ever going to sort it out?

CHAPTER THIRTEEN

'JUST tell her,' Mary said. 'Tell her what you told me when you thought I was asleep. Pretend *she's* asleep, if it helps.'

Sam's face flamed. 'Mum...'

She chuckled. 'I'm your mother, Sam. I might be old and frail, but that doesn't mean I've lost my marbles—or forgotten what it was like, being young.'

'You're not that old,' he said loyally.

'Old enough. And if I hadn't been too proud, too embarrassed to talk to the doctor when you were tiny...' She shook her head, her face crumpling. 'I'll never forgive myself for that,' she choked.

He took her hands. 'Don't, Mum. It was a long time ago, things were different then, and even if you'd taken me to see someone I'd probably still have had the same problem now.'

'Talk to her, Sam. Don't make the mistakes I made all through my life—all through *your* life.'

But I'm the same as you. Frosty when I get scared, Sam thought, and the words just stay inside my head. They won't come out.

'Tell her you love her and if she wants a baby you'll do whatever it takes. Follow your heart.'

And then everything's going to be all right? I hope so, Sam thought fervently. I hope so.

The best part of a week in Yorkshire, being spoiled by her parents and older brother—who, for once, hadn't tried to organise her life or make her talk about what was wrong—restored Jodie to the point where she could cope again.

When she returned to the ward, they were in the thick of things. The bronchiolitis epidemic seemed to have tailed off, with only one or two cases left, but Jodie found herself rushed off her feet with another transplant case, two fracture cases where abuse was suspected, a teenage overdose and a septicaemia case—the parents and carers all needed careful handling or long periods of counselling and explanation from her.

Once she'd have complained—albeit good-naturedly—of feeling drained at the end of her shift. Now she was grateful. Work kept her mind off Sam, who still hadn't returned, and she was too tired to do anything more than fall into bed when she got home at night. And that was just the way she liked it.

Until the day Sarah Ellis was admitted. The same day that Sam came back.

'Hello, Jodie.'

She almost dropped her notes at the sound of his voice. Part of her wanted to spin round and scream at him, demand to know why he thought she'd even be polite to him after the way he'd walked out on her, but the professional part of her won. Just.

'Sam,' she said coolly, not bothering to turn and face him.

'Jodie, I—we need to talk.'

'Not now. I'm with a patient.'

'Who's asleep,' he pointed out.

Jodie shrugged. 'I'm busy.'

'OK. When you're off duty, then.'

She shook her head. 'I don't think so, Sam.'

'Jodie—'

'As you once told me, *it'll pass.*' The sheer bitterness in her voice shocked even her.

He stared at her for a long, long moment.

She turned to face him, hoping that her eyes didn't betray how near she was to tears. 'We're colleagues, Sam. Just colleagues. End of story.'

It was a mistake, facing him. Seeing his face, his eyes that bleak Wednesday morning grey, the deep lines of strain etched into his face. He looked as if he hadn't slept properly for days. Wherever he'd been, whatever he'd been doing, it had taken its toll on him as much as it had on her.

But she couldn't reach out to him. Not now. Not when she knew that it would lead to yet another temporary truce, a truce that would last only until Sam's damaged heart told him to stay away from her again. And then he'd back off, leaving her lonely and aching and miserable with need. She couldn't go through that again.

'You look worried about your patient, Dr Price.'

Dr Price. After what had happened between them it was a mockery. But it was also the best way, she knew. No more hurt. Just colleagues. Keep their distance. Hadn't she told him that herself less than a minute ago?

She handed him the notes.

He read through them quickly, then whistled. 'Sanfilippo syndrome?' Sam looked at the sleeping child, then at Jodie. 'Rare. I'd imagine this must be the first case you've had on the ward.'

Jodie nodded.

'Have you come across it before?'

'No. There was a case in the hospital where I trained, but that was before my time.' She paused. 'I've been reading up on it.' Just like she'd read up on infertility. And this case was just as heartbreakingly hopeless.

'And?'

Clearly he'd switched into teaching mode and was expecting her to recite all the appropriate details. Well, that was something she could cope with. Anything to keep the emotional distance between them. Anything to stop her flinging herself into his arms and begging him to love her.

'It's a mucopolysaccharide disorder, first described in 1963 by Dr Sylvester Sanfilippo and also known as MPS-III; there are four different sub-types,' she recited. 'It's caused by a recessive gene and in the UK it's thought to affect around one in eighty-nine thousand people.'

'And what does that mean for Sarah?'

'She's missing an enzyme so her body can't break down the long chains of sugar molecules used in building the connective tissues. The sugars that haven't been broken down remain stored in the body and cause damage to the cells.' She sighed. 'There's currently a clinical trial in replacing the missing enzymes for MPS-I, but not Sanfilippo. Bone-marrow transplants haven't worked either, so at the moment there's no cure. She might live until her twenties, but probably not much later.'

Sam nodded. 'Symptoms?'

'It will get progressively worse, but we can't really give her parents much advice about which symptoms will occur and when, because some children are affected faster than others.' Jodie thought about what she'd read. 'There are three main stages—Sarah's at stage two. Her parents noticed that she was lagging behind in development, but she was always on the go and needed hardly any sleep. She didn't look any different to her friends—maybe a little smaller—and all preschoolers go through the "into everything" stage and chewing their hands, clothes and books. But they couldn't get her to be dry at night or by day—by the age of five, that's pretty rare—and they noticed recently that she's not talking as much as she did. She's very active, restless and what they called "a bit difficult". They wondered if she was hyperactive, but the tests were all negative. Their GP referred her to us and the blood and urine tests show she's Sanfilippo.'

'I had a Sanfilippo patient in London,' Sam said quietly. 'We referred her to Great Ormond Street, and I think we should do the same for Sarah. In the third phase, she'll slow down—she'll fall over a lot and become unsteady on her feet, then eventually lose her ability to walk.' He sat down on the edge of the little girl's bed and stroked her hair. 'Poor kid. She's going to have a tough time. And so are the parents. They'll have to cope with a growing child who's virtually immobile and won't be able to communicate with them.'

'They've got a new baby as well,' Jodie told him. 'They've asked for tests in case he's affected as well.'

'He's probably a carrier,' Sam said. 'There's a two in three chance that siblings of Sanfilippo patients will be carriers.'

'She's only in for tonight. To be honest, she didn't really need to stay in,' she admitted, 'but there was a bed free and I thought the parents could do with some time to come to terms with it. Not to mention get some sleep.'

'How long has Sarah been asleep?' Sam asked.

'An hour or so. Give it another couple of hours, and I think our whirlwind will be back,' Jodie said wryly. 'I've made an appointment for her parents to see a genetic counsellor.'

'Good idea. Do you know which form of Sanfilippo she has?'

'A, I think,' Jodie said. 'I know that B's sometimes milder and sufferers can live a relatively normal life into their twenties.'

'But that's not the case here,' Sam finished for her.

'I just hate not being able to do anything.' The words were out before she could stop them.

'We're doctors, but we're only human,' Sam told her softly. The same soft tone he'd used when he'd told her he loved her.

She forced the thought away.

'Every time I come across a case of, say, leukaemia,' he continued, 'see some bright, happy child that I know won't make it to twenty, I ask myself why I became a doctor, why we don't have a cure yet. And even when we do find a cure, it's going to be too late for that particular patient... I hate that part of our job, too. But we're doing the best we can.'

'Yes.' Jodie thought of the baby sister she'd had for just a few short days. 'If Sadie had been born now, she'd have had much more of a chance, with the medical advances over the last twenty-five years.'

On impulse, Sam reached out and squeezed her hand.

She flinched and pulled away.

'I'm sorry. I shouldn't have...' He sighed deeply. 'Go and get yourself a coffee, Dr Price. I think you need it.'

She forced herself to sound casual. 'Yes, boss.'

Jodie headed for the small kitchen at the back of the ward and put the kettle on. He was right, she knew—she needed a couple of minutes to get her emotions back under control. Emotions that were threatening to run way over the top. She'd been upset enough about her patient, but to have Sam walking back into her life, unannounced, saying they needed to talk...

But the time for talking was past. Long past.

*　　*　　*

Sam sat on the edge of the little girl's bed, staring at the notes without reading them. Maybe he should have stayed in Cornwall. Maybe he shouldn't have come back at all. Because Jodie wasn't going to give him the chance to explain anything.

He couldn't blame her. As far as she was concerned, he'd walked out on her after promising to be back—and he hadn't even spoken to her in the ten days he'd been away. He could protest his case, tell her how hard he'd tried to contact her, but she'd already judged him and passed sentence: deportation from her life.

But he was sure he'd seen something in her eyes when she'd looked at him. His mother's words echoed in his mind. *Tell her you love her... Follow your heart.*

And if she wouldn't talk to him, well, there were other ways.

'For me?' Jodie stared at the florist in surprise. It wasn't her birthday. Who on earth would send her flowers?

Her lips thinned as the answer hit her. Who else? 'Thank you, but I can't accept them,' she said tightly.

'I've got to deliver them, or my boss'll have my guts for garters,' the girl said, looking worried. 'Please?'

She didn't want the flowers—but she didn't want the girl to get the sack either. It wasn't *her* fault Sam was the biggest louse in history. 'OK. I'll sign,' she said. But the flowers were going to go straight into the bin.

Ten minutes later, she fished them out again. The hand-tied bouquet of roses and freesias was gorgeous, too beautiful to deserve dumping like that. She'd take it to the hospital for someone else to enjoy.

She wasn't curious about the card that came with them. Not a bit.

Not even the tiniest, tiniest bit...

She lasted nearly half an hour after putting the flowers in water before she opened the card. Two words, in Sam's black script. 'I'm sorry.'

Sorry for what? Walking out on her like that? Or sorry that it hadn't worked out? Well, she wasn't going to ask him. She didn't want to talk to him, other than on a professional basis. Though common courtesy dictated that she ought to write him a brief note of thanks.

As in just, 'Thanks for the flowers. Jodie.' She sealed it in an envelope and, just before she went on duty that afternoon, left it in his pigeonhole. The flowers went up to the geriatric ward—as Jodie told the sister in charge, 'To someone who'll enjoy them.'

Sam read the note and smiled. So communication was re-established. Grudging, but it was a start. She'd accepted his apology; now she might listen to the explanation. Or at least read it.

The next morning Jodie found a typed envelope with a Melbury postmark on her doormat. Junk mail? Or... Jodie frowned as she opened it to and found a photograph enclosed.

A photograph of an elderly woman she'd never seen before yet who looked familiar, particularly her grey eyes.

On the back, another note in Sam's handwriting. 'Mary Taylor.'

There was also a photocopy of a discharge sheet which also gave the date of Mary Taylor's admission for bacterial pneumonia. Jodie scanned it swiftly, worked out what Sam was trying to tell her and scowled. Well, now she knew where he'd been for those ten days—and why.

So why the hell hadn't he called her and told her what was happening? Why had he just left her in limbo like that?

She replaced the photograph and discharge sheet in the envelope and shoved it in a kitchen drawer. She wasn't even going to dignify this with a reply.

The next day, she had an email from Sam. *Patient recommendation.* Work, this time. OK, she could deal with that. Except the text of the message was blank—there was just an attachment. *Recommendation.doc.* Well, thanks, Sam, she fumed inwardly. That tells me a lot— I don't think. Who's the patient? What's the case?

She opened it and her eyes widened in shock. He'd sent her an article on the latest research about artificial insemination by donor.

Patient recommendation?

Enough was enough. She stomped down the corridor to his office.

'Is he in?' she asked Julianne.

'Yes, but—'

Jodie ignored Julianne's 'he's busy' and marched straight in, slamming the door shut behind her to forestall any interruptions. Dragon, beware, she thought—right now she could out-dragon anyone!

Sam looked up from his paperwork. 'Dr Price.'

She folded her arms. 'Stop playing games with me.'

'Games?'

'The flowers, the photograph, the email—just stop.'

He spread his hands. 'What else was I supposed to do? You weren't talking to me.'

'Are you surprised?'

He sighed. 'No. But give me five minutes to explain.'

'One.'

'Three.'

She wasn't in the mood for negotiating. 'Fifty-five seconds, starting now.'

'The hospital in Cornwall rang to say my mother had been admitted with pneumonia and was asking for me, so I didn't even stop to think—I just drove straight down there. I stopped on the way to ring you and explain but you were out and you don't have an answering machine.' He grimaced. 'Or if you do it wasn't switched on. I kept ringing and you didn't answer. I rang you at work and you were too busy to talk to me—with patients, with parents, away from the ward. I asked Julianne to tell you to ring me urgently. You didn't. I rang again and she said you were on leave.' He sighed again. 'I didn't know where you were or how to reach you. So I stayed with Mum, settled her in for a couple of days after she was discharged and came straight back to you.'

That explained why he'd looked so tired at Sarah Ellis's bedside. He'd just driven for eight hours or so—to come straight to her.

'And you made it clear you weren't going to discuss anything with me.'

'Do you blame me?' she snapped.

'I don't exactly have a good track record when it comes to talking things over,' he admitted wryly. 'But we need to talk, Jodie.'

'There's nothing to talk about.'

'Isn't there?'

'Your fifty-five seconds are up.'

'And?'

'And nothing!' She stomped out of the room again.

It was only when she was halfway down the corridor that Sam's words sank in. He'd asked Julianne to tell her to ring him yet Julianne hadn't passed on the message.

Her eyes narrowed. Why hadn't Julianne tried to find her to give her the message? Or she could have paged her or put a note with her post? Was she in love with Sam? Or was she just on some kind of power trip, trying to prove her importance to the team?

Not that it mattered. Because Jodie was not—definitely *not*—going to get involved with Sam Taylor ever again.

Though it nagged at her for the rest of the day. Patient recommendation. Was Sam trying to tell her that he'd come round to her way of thinking, that he was prepared to try AID if and when they decided they wanted children?

Stop, she told herself firmly. He's going away. And you're going to get over him. Not now, not tomorrow, not next year—but some day.

Later that evening, on his way out of the ward, Sam stopped dead in his tracks. He knew that voice. Except this time it wasn't singing a version of Incey Wincey Spider. This time it was singing an old-fashioned lullaby. 'Golden slumbers seal your eyes, Smiles awake you when you rise...'

He couldn't resist it. Even though he knew he should be dealing with the mountain of paperwork in his in-tray—and even though he knew he should keep away from Jodie—he walked as if spellbound towards that voice and leaned on the doorjamb.

She was cradling a small baby in her arms, one of the last bronchiolitis victims. Baby Madison had touched all their hearts because her fifteen-year-old mother had decided to give her up for adoption and refused to spend any time with the baby. Most of the nursing staff spent a few minutes each day talking to her and letting her hold their fingers, and some of them had gone as far as Jodie, cuddling her during feeds and generally making a fuss of her, giving her the affection her natural mother wasn't offering her.

Jodie was born to be a mother. The way she was cradling the sick infant, holding her so gently and stroking the soft little cheek… It was how she'd be with her own baby. The baby he desperately wanted with her.

And he'd left it too late. He'd thrown it all away.

He gave a choked sound and her head whipped up. She stared at him, eyes dilated, and he backed away.

'Sam?'

Her voice was clear and it echoed in the quiet of the evening ward—most visitors had left by now.

'I'm sorry. I know what you said. Just colleagues.'

'That's right.'

Was it his imagination, or was there a slight quiver in her voice?

Well, there was only one way to find out. And this, he knew, was definitely his last chance. 'Jodie. There's something I need to say to you.' he said softly. 'Please.'

'I'm on duty.' Her voice was steady as she put Baby Madison back in her cot, checked the monitor leads and tubes, and gently placed a sheet over her.

'It won't take long. Maybe it's too little, too late—but, please, hear me out.'

She faced him, unsmiling.

'We never talked in my family. I don't know why—it was just the way we were. I didn't get the chance to tell my father how much I loved him.' He bit his lip. 'Dad died of a heart attack when I was a student. I didn't get there in time for the end. So when I heard my mother was in hospital, I had to go. I didn't know how ill she was and I didn't want to make the same mistake again.'

She said nothing, but he could see the slight film of tears misting her green eyes.

'I thought my mother was asleep and I started talking to her—talking to her the way I'd always wanted to but never had. I told her about this woman I'd met. A woman with the eyes of an angel. How she was the most beautiful woman I'd ever seen. Everyone loved her and I wanted her more than anything in the world, but I couldn't give her the one thing she wanted. Babies.

'And then I found out my mother hadn't been asleep at all. She told me to tell you what I'd just said to her— pretend you were asleep if I had to.'

'Pretend I was asleep?' Jodie frowned, not following Sam's reasoning.

'So I could find the right words.' His mouth quirked wryly. 'I'm no good at talking. You know that. I just freeze and the words won't come out.'

There was nothing she could say to that.

'And she told me to follow my heart.' He spread his hands. 'You were right all along. There are lots of things we could do. If we had a baby with the help of a donor...' He took a deep breath. 'Look at Baby Madison here. She'll grow up with a mother who isn't her biological mother and a father who isn't her biological father—but they'll still be her parents and they'll still love her because she's *their* child. They'll have chose her, so she's special to them. Just as our child would be special to us.'

'Our child.' Jodie's throat worked convulsively. 'And that's the be-all and end-all, isn't it? A baby.'

He shook his head. 'If we're lucky enough to have children, that'd be the icing on the cake. But...' He raked a hand through his hair. 'Look, I don't want to finish this conversation in the middle of a hospital ward.'

'I'm on duty.'

'We need to talk,' Sam said. 'As from now, we're both off duty.'

'But—'

'But nothing. Your bike stays here, you come with me, and we're going somewhere a bit more private.'

'The ward's quiet enough tonight.'

'According to the duty roster, you should have left two hours ago and I'm supposedly several hundred miles away.' He smiled wryly. 'Though I know why you're still here. From what I've heard, I think everyone on the ward wants to adopt this little one.'

Was he suggesting…? Her green eyes were huge as she stared at him. 'Sam, I didn't—'

'There's only one way to stop you talking, Jodie Price,' he cut in. 'And that's this.' He curved one hand round her neck and touched his lips gently to hers.

After that first touch, the kiss turned explosive, and it was only when there was a loud cough behind them that they broke apart.

'Madison's monitor is going mad,' Fiona pointed out. 'And the two doctors in her room—consultant and registrar at that, I might add—are completely ignoring it, so I suppose the nursing staff will have to do something about it.'

'I…' Jodie flushed.

'Get her out of here, Sam Taylor, and sort it out. Pronto,' Fiona directed.

'Funny, I thought scary matrons who bossed doctors about died out years ago,' Sam muttered.

'I heard that,' Fiona said, checking the monitor resetting it and adjusting the cuff around the baby's foot. 'Go. The pair of you. And don't come back until you've got some good news for us, do you hear?'

'Yes, ma'am.' Sam took Jodie's hand and tugged her out of the room.

CHAPTER FOURTEEN

'WHERE are we going?'

'Somewhere quiet.'

Why had she even bothered asking? Sam was going frosty on her again. Or maybe... Hadn't he said something about the words not coming out, even though he wanted to say them? And he was still holding her hand. Holding it tightly, as if it were the only thing keeping him from drowning.

Jodie decided not to break the silence—when he was ready, Sam would talk.

Eventually, she realised where they were heading—through the cathedral close and down to the river, to the place where he'd first told her he couldn't have children and they had no future.

Her heart gave a sick lurch. Surely he wasn't going to do that again? Surely not, after the way he'd kissed her at the baby's bedside?

Make it be all right this time, she prayed silently. Please. Please. Don't let it all go wrong now.

At last they reached the bench where they'd parted so harshly before, now bathed in the glow from a streetlamp. Sam sat down and pulled her onto his lap.

'I find it so hard to talk—so hard to tell you how I really feel. So don't interrupt me now,' he warned, his face serious in the lamplight. 'Just hear me out.

'I love you. I love you more than anyone I've ever met. I think I've been in love with you since the day I met you, though I tried to keep away. After Angela, I swore I'd never get involved with anyone again, never give someone the chance to reject me because I'm not physically perfect.'

Not physically perfect? When he was the most gorgeous man she'd ever laid eyes on? Jodie was itching to jump in and tell him, but he'd asked her to hear him out. So she waited. Just.

'I didn't want to get hurt—but I couldn't stop thinking about you. When you asked me to Mario's, I wasn't going to turn up. But I found myself there, waiting for you. The Christmas party was even worse—I nearly kissed you in front of everyone.'

'And Christmas Day…' she said softly.

'I thought I'd died and gone to heaven. It felt so right, sleeping with you in my arms. I never wanted to let you go. I was on early the next morning. I thought you deserved your sleep, so I didn't wake. I left you a note.'

'It fell down between the bed and my bedside cabinet. I didn't see it.'

He nodded. 'And you didn't answer the phone when I rang you from the ward.'

'I was on my way to Yorkshire.'

'I didn't know that then. I assumed you were already having second thoughts and had just ignored the phone. The more I thought about it, the more I was convinced it would never work out between us. It'd be unfair to raise your hopes of ever having your own children when I knew I couldn't give you a baby. I had to walk away, for your sake.' He smiled. 'Except I couldn't. When you kissed me in my office, I lost it completely. I couldn't help myself. The same thing happened at your house. Whenever you touch me, I go up in flames. I've never lost control like that with anyone in my life before, and it scares me,' he admitted frankly.

'I'd never hurt you, Sam,' she said softly.

'I know. I know *now*,' he amended. 'And then my mother was ill. She was asking for me, she's on her own, and I couldn't just abandon her, Jodie.'

'Of course not.' She'd have thought a great deal less of him if he had.

'I tried ringing you but I couldn't get hold of you. I asked Julianne to tell you to ring me, but you didn't.'

Jodie coughed. 'She, um, didn't pass on the message.'

'What?' Sam stared at her. 'But…she's normally so efficient.'

Not to mention being a dragon. Jodie shrugged. 'Maybe she was trying to protect you.'

'Protect me?' he echoed.

'Duncan calls her Cerberus,' she elaborated.

Sam's lips twitched. 'Which makes my office Hades.'

Jodie chuckled. 'I never thought of that. A snowflake's chance in hell, hmm?'

He smiled back, then suddenly sobered. 'These last few days I thought I'd left it too late. Being without you has been torture.'

'You don't have to be without me any more.'

'What about children? We can't just ignore the question and pretend it's not there. Infertility's a big thing, Jodie. If you—' he almost choked on the words '—you don't think you can handle it, I'll understand if you bow out now.'

'I don't have any answers. I don't know how I'm going to feel when my biological clock starts ticking.' She bit her lip. 'Ellen says I'm just ducking the issue. But we can face it when we come to it. Together. Whatever happens now, I want to be with you. That's what really matters, you and me.' She paused. 'Baby Madison…'

He stroked her cheek. 'Baby Madison is gorgeous—but she's already got a couple lined up to adopt her.'

Jodie blinked. 'Since when?'

'Yesterday morning.' He coughed. 'I, um, made a few enquiries.'

'You made enquiries?' she asked, surprised.

He nodded. 'It was just a crazy idea. Something that didn't work out.'

Was he saying he'd been prepared to adopt Baby Madison for her? He loved her that much? 'There'll be other Madisons,' Jodie said gently.

'I know.' He paused. 'I've applied to work abroad.'

'You've done *what*?' He'd told her he was going, but...*abroad*? Surely he couldn't mean it. Not when he'd just said he loved her and being without her was torture. He couldn't leave now. He *couldn't*.

'I couldn't handle working with you. Not when I wanted to hold you and kiss you and lose myself in your delectable body.' He laughed ruefully. 'You proved that to me in my office. Not to mention your house. I have no self-control when you're around.'

'You're not really going ahead with it, are you?'

'I don't know.'

A lump formed in her throat. 'What would make you change your mind and stay?' she asked carefully.

'You.' Sam shifted so that he was kneeling in front of her, completely disregarding the cold, wet, muddy grass surrounding the bench, or the fact that it had just started to snow. 'I didn't want to ask you in the middle of the ward, with an audience. Just in case you...' He stopped. 'I thought here—here, where I made the biggest mistake of my life—is the place to put things right between us again. I know I don't talk when I should do but I'll do my best to reform. I swear it.'

'How do you mean, reform?' she asked.

'Learn to discuss my feelings. It'll take time and I need someone—well, a certain someone—to take me in hand and teach me how. Jodie Price, will you please take pity on me and be my lawful wedded wife?'

She stared at him, not sure she'd heard him correctly.

The pause lengthened, and eventually he sighed and stood up. 'OK. I'm sorry. I blew it. I'll take you home.'

'Wait!' Jodie scrambled to her feet. 'Did you just ask me to…marry you?'

'Yes.' His voice was cracked.

'Whether we have children or not?' she tested.

He nodded. 'I want you, Jodie, more than I've ever wanted anyone in my whole life. And if you decide you want a baby, then we'll try whatever it takes to give us a child. Whether it's adoption, fostering, sperm donation—there are lots of things we could try. We'll find something that works for us, if and when *you're* ready. Because, babies or not, I don't want to spend the rest of my life without you. It wouldn't be living—it'd be just existing, in some grey and dull place. I want to be with you, Jodie. I want to wake up with you every morning. I want your face to be the last thing I see every night. The words don't even begin to say what I feel about you but…I love you, Jodie. I really, really love you.'

So he meant it, then. He really did feel the same way as she did.

'I'm not dreaming?' she questioned, still not quite sure she could believe her ears.

'Dreaming what?'

'You love me, and we're going to be together?'

Sam nodded. 'I love you. And we're going to be together—when you agree to marry me, that is.'

She chuckled. 'When, hmm?'

'Are you going to keep me in suspense for much longer?' he demanded.

'Ooh...' She pretended to consider it, still laughing, then sobered. 'Sam. You've been through all this before. You know, looking at ways to have a baby. With Angela.' She swallowed. 'I know it sounds as if I'm prying, and I really don't mean it to, but...what happened? And can you really bear to go through it all again? I mean, if it's going to just rip open old wounds for you, much as I want a baby, I'd rather not go down that route. It wouldn't be fair on you.'

He stroked her cheek. 'You're the one who's always reminding me you're not Angela.'

'I mean it, Sam. You've been hurt enough already. I don't want to add to that, stir up all the bad memories. I love you too much to put you through the mill again.'

He bit his lip. 'A lot of people who go through fertility treatment end up splitting up. The thing you both want most in the world ends up tearing you apart.'

'It doesn't have to be like that for us.'

'No. I know. Just because it happened before—'

'Doesn't mean it'll happen again,' she finished.

He sighed. 'It's not pleasant—though it's probably going to be worse for you than it is for me, being poked and prodded and asked never-ending and very, very intimate questions. You can forget about dignity—by the time all the investigations are over you don't have any left. And when you've done all that, the results seem to take for ever to arrive.'

She squeezed his hand. 'It must have been hard, seeing it written down in black and white that you couldn't have children.'

'I didn't actually see it,' Sam admitted.

Jodie frowned. 'What do you mean?'

'Angela opened the results. Then she shredded them. Well, she was upset,' he said. 'It was her way of dealing with it. I wasn't going to make it worse by ringing the lab to ask for another bit of paper.'

'So you didn't actually see what the results said?'

'Angela wasn't a medic, but she wouldn't have mis-read them, if that's what you're thinking,' Sam said.

Jodie's eyes narrowed. 'Does she have any children now?'

He shrugged. 'I've no idea. We didn't stay in touch. The divorce was handled by my solicitor. She didn't con-test it and I…I didn't see her again.'

A tiny piece of hope sprang up in her heart. 'Are you really sure she told you the truth?'

Sam frowned. 'Why would she lie about something like that?'

'You said she left you for her boss. Maybe she used that as an excuse,' Jodie suggested.

He shook his head. 'Things were bad between us to-wards the end, but she wouldn't do something as horrible as that. But if I wasn't infertile, why didn't we…? Oh.' It suddenly dawned on him. 'You think she might have been the one with problems?'

'You might have reduced fertility, Sam, but if she had problems as well—problems she didn't tell you about, such as endometriosis or scarring of her tubes from an operation in her past—then that's why she didn't con-ceive.' Jodie bit her lip. 'It might not have been you. At least, not *just* you.' Which meant that she and Sam had more of a chance of having their own child. The hope flared brighter. 'Could your condition change, do you think?'

Sam shook his head. 'I don't see how. Besides, fertility decreases with age, doesn't it?'

'But neither of us are fertility specialists,' Jodie pointed out. 'Sam...I know it's a horrible thing to ask, but would you—would you check it out? Get a copy of the letter from your consultant so we know exactly what we're dealing with?'

He sighed. 'It's not going to change anything, but OK. If that's what you want, we'll do it.' He kissed the tip of her nose. 'Don't tell me you're going to be a reformed character yourself and keep a neat file on all this,' he teased.

She grinned back, not in the least offended. 'Well...'

'Jodie, the results might still be the same,' he said, 'which rules out IVF. AID might not work, and the authorities might hold my age against us when it comes to adoption.'

'You're only—what, thirty-five?'

'Yes, but there's a cut-off point somewhere,' he warned, 'and then there's all the admin and assessments to go through first to check if we're suitable. At the end of it all, we still might not have a baby. We might go through months and months of waiting and hoping and heartache for nothing.'

Jodie's eyes were huge as she looked at him. 'I know. Adoption's only one of the things we can look at.' She paused. 'But at the end of it all, if none of them work, we've still got each other. That's the important thing.'

'Have we?' he asked.

'Have we what?'

'Got each other? You still haven't actually said you'll marry me,' he reminded her.

She smiled. 'Yes.'

'Yes?' he prompted.

'OK, if you insist on being pedantic, yes, Sam Taylor, I love you and, yes, Sam Taylor, I will marry you.'

He pulled her into his arms and kissed her thoroughly. By the time he lifted his head, she was shaking.

'Cold?' He brushed a snowflake from her cheek.

'Yes—no—yes. I don't know.' She laughed. 'I can't think straight with you around.'

'I know the feeling. Good, isn't it?' He kissed her again. 'I think it's called happiness.'

'Happiness.' Jodie smiled. 'There was a point when I didn't think I'd ever be happy again—when I thought you'd left me.'

'I know, and I'm sorry. I've got a lot of making up to do to you,' he said.

She grinned. 'I'll hold you to that.'

She was quiet for a long time while he kissed her. When they resurfaced, her eyes were shining with tears— this time, tears of joy.

'I love you, Sam,' she said softly. 'Baby or no baby. I want to spend the rest of my life with you.'

'Nothing's ever going to part us again,' he promised.

'Ever,' she echoed. 'Let's go home. I thought coffee…or something.'

He smiled back. 'Define something.'

Her smile broadened and she traced his lower lip with her forefinger. 'I don't think I need to—do I?'

Two weeks later, Jodie finished dressing. 'Do I look all right?' she asked nervously, looking at herself in the long mirror.

'Yes!' came the chorus from her mother, Ellen, Annie and Fiona.

'I still can't believe you're getting married,' Ellen said. 'This quickly.'

'Not to mention beating Matt and me down the aisle,' Annie teased.

'There wasn't any point in waiting,' Jodie said. 'We wanted the rest of our lives to start right now. And hardly anyone gets married at this time of year, so it was easy to book the venue.' She smiled ruefully. 'I'm sorry about letting you down with the big church wedding, Mum. But Sam couldn't get married in church anyway, so this is the next best thing.'

'It's absolutely fine, as long as you're both happy. And you look beautiful,' her mother said, blinking away a tear.

Jodie had one eye on her watch. 'We'd better go downstairs.'

'Another first,' Fiona said. 'A doctor on time.'

'Oh, ha, ha,' Jodie said, but she was beaming from ear to ear. In only a few minutes she was going to walk into the hall of the beautiful old country house on her father's arm—and she was going to be married to Sam.

The last two weeks had been crazy. Her parents had been shocked and then delighted, especially when Sam had rung them later to ask formal permission for Jodie's hand in marriage. Matt, for once in his life, had been silenced. Ellen had simply stared and stared when Jodie had called round to ask if she fancied being a matron of honour, with Billy as page-boy. And Sam's mother's whoop of joy when they rung her with the news had been so loud that even Jodie, who'd been sitting on Sam's lap as he'd talked, had been able to hear it.

The morning after Sam's proposal, they'd gone into work together. Fiona had been there before them and had noted their arrival.

'Well?' she asked, hands on hips and her mouth compressed into a hard line.

'Well, what, Sister?' Sam asked coolly.

'Are you two finally seeing sense?'

'Probably not,' Sam said. 'But I need to see you later about something, Sister Ferguson. Something extremely important.' He gave her a sidelong look, then a huge grin and kissed Jodie soundly. 'And you, my love, have things to do this morning.'

'Mmm.' Jodie touched the tip of his nose with her finger. 'See you at lunchtime.'

He whispered something in her ear that made her laugh and blush. She gave Fiona a wink, then went home to make a few calls.

When Jodie returned to the ward at lunchtime to meet Sam, she caught various people whispering in huddles, but no one said a word to her. She found out what the whispers were about after lunch when Sam had whisked her into one of the most exclusive jewellers in Melbury to buy a simple solitaire diamond set in platinum. When they walked back onto the ward, there were congratulatory notices everywhere—drawn and decorated by the patients who could hold a pencil, with the handprints of various babies and those who were too sick to write. There was a huge table of canapés at the nurses' station, champagne for those about to go off duty and orange juice for those who weren't.

'I…' Jodie gave up, overwhelmed, and just beamed at everyone.

'Couldn't happen to a nicer couple,' Fiona said, hugging them both.

'But— When did all this…?'

'His credit card, my talent for organisation,' Fiona said with a wink, nodding at Sam. 'Come on, then, let's see the ring.'

They pulled a similar stunt the day before the wedding, decorating the ward with bows and papier-mâché bells, courtesy of the more active children on the ward. Jodie had changed the traditional bridal favours into goodie bags for the patients and boxes of Belgian chocolate sea-shells for her colleagues, and promised to bring in the photographs to show everyone.

And now she and Sam were about to take the final step... She shivered.

'Second thoughts?' her mother murmured.

'Never,' Jodie said softly. 'Just nervous.'

'You'll be fine.' Her mother hugged her. 'Now, stop it, or you'll *really* make me cry!'

As the string quartet began to play 'The Arrival of the Queen of Sheba', Sam turned to face his bride. Stunning barely began to describe her. She wore a slim-fitting ivory raw silk dress with a kick-pleat at the back, and her hair was pinned up in a way that reminded him of the young Grace Kelly. As she came closer, he realised that there were pearls in her hair—presumably some sort of posh hairpins. Her bouquet was a very simple arrange-ment of ivory roses and gypsophila, and walking behind her he saw Ellen in a simple lavender raw silk shift dress, Billy in a sailor suit and little Amy Simcox toddling along next to him in a smaller version of Ellen's dress, slightly unsteady and clutching Billy's hand.

Tears pricked at the backs of his eyes. Amy Simcox, the toddler Jodie had sung to and played with while she'd been in traction. Jodie had gone round to see her after the splints had been taken off, taking a couple of toys to help encourage her to walk. Amy, the sick child who'd started this whole thing off. It was fitting that she should be their bridesmaid. Trust Jodie to think of that.

Everyone in the rows of seats in the ballroom stood up as Jodie approached, then sat down again as the reg-istrar began his speech. By the time he informed Sam they were man and wife and the string quartet played Pachelbel's 'Canon', there was hardly a dry eye in the room.

'And now,' Sam said, 'I'm going to kiss the bride.' And he did.

'I don't think I've ever seen a more radiant bride,' Ellen said.

Jodie just grinned broadly at her best friend.

Ellen tipped her head on one side. 'I recognise that look. Is there something else you're not telling me? Like...you're going to make me a godmother?'

Jodie shook her head. 'Not quite. We're working on it, though. Sam's written to the clinic that treated him, asking for copies of all the test results and his records. He's going to have another test, too—what seemed impossible a few years ago might be something we can work with now. You know how quickly medicine advances.' Her eyes sparkled. 'But for the moment I'm just enjoying having Sam all to myself.'

Ellen chuckled. 'From the look on his face, he's having similar thoughts.'

Jodie glanced towards her new husband, who was in earnest conversation with her father. As if he knew she was looking at him, he lifted his head to catch her gaze and smiled at her. The sheer love in his face made her feel as if she were walking on air. Happiness, she thought. Even if they never managed to have a baby, they'd still have this. Always.

Several hours later, when Sam and Jodie were dancing cheek to cheek, he turned to whisper in her ear. 'Happy?'

'Very. You?'

'Uh-huh. I'd rate this as the second-best day of my life.'

'Second-best?' Did that mean his first wedding day had been better? Jodie tensed.

He dropped a kiss on the end of her nose. 'It's going to take a lot to beat Melbury cathedral on a winter night, with snow falling and you accepting my proposal of marriage.'

'Oh.' She relaxed.

'Mum agrees with me about you,' he told her. 'You're the most beautiful woman in the world and you have the eyes of an angel.'

'Flatterer!' She grinned. 'I'm sorry Dad and Matt gave you a grilling.'

'Only natural. They love you very much.' He paused. 'They were a bit easier than your mum and Ellen.'

'Ah.'

'I think they all just wanted to be sure of my intentions.'

'Which are?'

'To make this the best and happiest marriage in history,' he said simply. 'I love you, Jodie.' He kissed the curve of her neck. 'Do you reckon anyone would notice if we slipped away?'

'Only your mum, my parents, Matt and Annie, Ellen, Fiona and the rest of the ward,' she retorted, laughing.

'Worth a try, though,' he said, edging her towards the door. 'Because, right now, I can't wait to have you all to myself...'

CHAPTER FIFTEEN

'I CAN'T be.' Jodie stared at her GP in a mixture of shock and delight just over two months later. 'I can't be.' It was impossible—wasn't it?

'All your symptoms add up. Have you done a test?'

Jodie shook her head.

'We can do one here, but you might just as well use a home testing kit. They're as accurate as the ones we use and you'll get the confirmation now instead of tomorrow morning.'

'So, how pregnant am I?' she asked.

'About ten weeks, I'd say,' the doctor said sagely. 'We'll send you for a scan to check.'

'But…' Sam didn't think his condition could have changed. How could she possibly be pregnant? And to be ten weeks pregnant—that meant she'd conceived on their honeymoon. In Venice, the most gorgeous city in the world. Not that they'd explored many of the sights. They'd taken advantage of the dark evenings to have early nights. Not to mention afternoon naps… Her lips curved at the memory.

They'd never once used protection, assuming they hadn't had to. And she'd had a period since they'd come home. A very light one. Earlier than she'd expected. Her next one had been missing altogether, but she'd put that down to rushing about—that and the occasional bit of nausea. And she'd put that down to nerves about some forthcoming exams. It was the stuff of family legend that Jodie was sick when she was nervous, and she'd actually thrown up over her examiner's feet on the morning of her driving test. Had she been wrong and it had been morning sickness instead?

She'd been feeling tired lately, too. She'd just assumed she was a bit run-down, so she'd come to her GP to check her iron levels. And now he was telling her she wasn't anaemic or run-down, she was expecting a baby—the baby they'd thought they'd never have.

She couldn't quite take it in.

They were going to have a baby—a baby of their own?

'Is anything wrong, Jodie?'

Jodie shook her head. 'I'm just a bit stunned, that's all.'

'A happy accident, hmm?'

'Yes.' Yes, yes, yes! She smiled. 'Something like that.' But before she could tell Sam, there were a couple of things she needed to do. On impulse, she reached over and kissed her GP. 'This is better than, oh, all my birthdays and Christmases and everything rolled into one.'

'Well, congratulations,' her GP said warmly. 'And before you go, we'll book you in for your antenatal appointments.'

Antenatal appointments. Jodie hugged herself. Just wait until Sam heard the news—he was going to be a dad! This would really knock him for six.

'So, did the GP say you've been overdoing it and you need iron tablets, then?' Sam asked as he walked into the kitchen, later that evening, to find his wife sitting with her feet up on a chair.

'No. I'm OK.'

'Hmm. I still think you're studying too hard.'

'I'll slow down,' Jodie promised. She had a feeling that, once Sam knew, she wouldn't have a choice in the matter! 'Stop worrying. Everything's fine.' More than fine, but there was something else she wanted him to see before she told him her news. Something she'd found lying on the doormat when she'd returned from the doctor's.

Fed up with the endless wait for the paperwork to come back from Sam's previous specialist—who'd retired and the results had apparently been archived, so it would take a long time to retrieve them—she'd persuaded Sam to go for another test. A test whose results now lay in the brown envelope she was holding. Had she not already guessed what it had to say, she'd have probably taken the envelope straight to Sam's office and made him open it. As it was, she'd been confident enough to wait for him to come off duty. 'Um, this came for you in the second post.' She waved the envelope at him. 'Open it.'

He heard the impatient note in her voice and frowned. 'What?'

'It's from the clinic. Look at the franking,' Jodie said. 'Come on, open it! Let's see what they have to tell us.'

'You could have opened it,' he said.

'Not on your life.' Someone had read his results once before—and Jodie knew for certain now that Angela had got it wrong. This time there would be no mistake. She wanted Sam to see it himself in black and white.

The truth.

'Are you going to open that envelope or not?'

He nodded. 'In a minute.'

'Sam? Don't freeze on me now. *Talk* to me. I'm your wife, remember? And you promised to reform,' she pointed out.

'Yes.' He sighed. 'Sorry. It's— I suppose it's a bit like opening your exam results. Except I always had a pretty good idea how I'd done in my exams, whereas this...

I don't know. I've got no control over it. And it scares me, Jodie. What if…?' His voice tailed off.

'Whatever it says, I love you,' she informed him firmly. 'Now and always. That's not going to change, whether you can have babies or not. I love you, Sam Taylor, for keeps. OK?'

'OK.' He gave her a nervous smile, then slit the envelope. He read the short letter in silence. Then he read it again. Then he read it a third time, just in case he'd got it wrong. And then he dropped the letter on the table, picked Jodie up and whirled her round in his arms.

'Good news, I take it?' she asked in amusement when he'd put her down.

'The best! Jodie, either something's changed or Angela got it wrong. Maybe she thought subfertile meant infertile—I don't know. Apparently, I've a very low sperm count, but the motility's fine.' He whirled her round again and laughed. 'Which means that if we want to try it, ICSI should work for us.'

'That's fantastic news.' She kissed him.

'All this time… All this time I thought I couldn't have children, and I've put you through hell over it. I'm so sorry.'

'That's in the past,' she said firmly. 'I think we need some champagne. To celebrate.' Well, *he* could have the champagne. She would have just a tiny sip.

'Definitely.' Sam rubbed his nose against hers. 'We're going to be parents, Jodie. We really, really are.'

If she didn't tell him soon she'd burst! But she'd promised herself this. She wanted to see his face as he worked it out for himself—that she already knew the results of his tests before she'd even seen them. 'Oh, before I forget, I've got a present for you.'

'Present?' His eyes widened. 'I haven't forgotten an anniversary or anything, have I?'

'No.' Sam bought her flowers every month to celebrate the day she'd agreed to marry him, a gesture which still delighted her. And there were one or two more private dates they celebrated in other ways. 'It's— I suppose you could call it a late wedding present,' she said. 'A late honeymoon present even.'

He frowned. 'I'm not with you.'

She handed him a small package. 'Here.'

His frown deepened. 'What is it?'

'Open it,' she said mysteriously.

Sam did so—and gazed in surprise at the paintbrush. 'What's this for?'

'There's something else with it.' She turned the brush round in his hands so he could see the plain brown envelope taped to the bristles.

He opened it and just stared at the narrow white stick. 'Jodie?'

'Turn it the other way round and read it,' she said.

With shaking hands, he did so—and noted the blue line in the two windows. 'Jodie...' He lifted stunned eyes to hers. 'Is this—is this what I think it is?'

'Yep.'

'You're pregnant.' He looked as stunned as she'd felt when her GP had told her the news.

'Which is why I've been feeling so tired. Not because I've been studying too hard. And that's why I've been feeling sick, too—morning sickness, not exam nerves.' She smiled. 'The GP examined me, but I did the test just to make sure. We've got a scan booked for the week after next.'

'How—how long?'

'Ten weeks, apparently—which makes this a Venetian

baby.' She grinned broadly. 'If you weren't so heavy, I think I'd spin *you* round the kitchen!'

'We're going to have a baby.' He stared at the test stick, then at his wife. 'Jodie—we're going to have a *baby*!' His eyes glistened with tears. 'I can't believe it. We're actually going to have a baby. You're carrying—' his voice was hushed with awe '—my child.'

'Hence the brush. You've got some decorating to do. Our baby's nursery,' she clarified with a grin. 'Lemon yellow. Though we could use blue as we're obviously having a boy.'

'Who says? It's definitely a girl,' he retorted. 'A girl as beautiful as her mother.'

'Ha.' She hugged him. 'It's been killing me, keeping this quiet since lunchtime. I nearly rang you about twenty times to tell you—only I didn't dare ask Julianne to put me through.'

'As if you're scared of anyone.' He kissed her again. 'I can't quite take this in. We're having a baby... Oh, heavens. You haven't been rushing around on your bike, have you?'

Jodie looked slightly evasive. 'Not since lunchtime.'

'I'm locking it up. I know what you're like. From now on, I'm going to be your taxi service. No cycling, no rushing round, no overdoing things. And why are you standing up? You should be resting!' He sat down at the table and pulled her onto his lap.

'Stop fussing. I'm perfectly healthy.' She tangled one hand in his hair. 'Just...pregnant.'

'Pregnant.' He savoured the word and stroked her still flat abdomen. 'Pregnant with our baby.'

'Are you...pleased?' she asked diffidently.

'*Pleased?*' Sam swallowed hard. 'That doesn't even begin to cover it. I thought—I thought we'd have to wait for months. The results of my test today...well, that gave us an extra option—IVF. But it all takes so long. I never dreamed we'd have a child of our own so soon.' He shook his head. 'I'm shocked, I'm excited, I'm scared, I...I want to climb up on the roof and tell the whole world I'm going to be a dad!' Words he'd never thought he'd ever, ever be able to say. Six little words. *We're going to have a baby.*

'Not a good idea,' Jodie said, taking the pregnancy test and paintbrush from his hand and putting them on top of the letter from the clinic.

He stared at her, his skin prickling. 'Why not? Everything's all right, isn't it? I mean, you're not— Our baby— I...' Fear bubbled up through his words.

'Stop worrying. You'll drive me insane if you're like this for the next thirty weeks.' She kissed the tip of his nose. 'All I meant was, if you fell off the roof, you'd be in plaster for months, and I want you at antenatal classes with me.'

'Just you try stopping me! I'll be there at every single appointment. I'll learn how to give you a proper back rub, I'll do all the breathing with you, and you can swear at me all you like while you're in transition. I love you, Dr Taylor.' His eyes turned silver. 'You *and* our baby.'

'And I love you.' She nuzzled his cheek. 'Though I'd kill for a Margherita pizza with avocado.'

He grinned. 'In anyone else, that'd be a craving. In you, that's normal.'

'Actually, I do have a craving.' Her lips twitched. 'Two.'

'Name them,' he said instantly. 'They're yours.'

'A bowl of cornflakes with ice-cold milk, no sugar.'

'And the second?'

She pursed her lips. 'I want to eat them in bed. Next to a certain dark-haired, grey-eyed doctor.'

He gave her a sidelong look. 'How about a rain check on the cornflakes?'

'And a very, very private celebration before we tell the rest of the world?' she suggested.

'It's a deal.' He kissed her, then swung her into his arms and carried her out of the kitchen.

EPILOGUE

SAM sat on his wife's bed and cradled their sleeping baby in his arms. 'I can hardly believe he's ours—he's really here,' he said, his voice hushed.

'How did we create something so perfect?' Jodie asked with a smile, reaching out to hold the baby's tiny fingers. 'I could watch him for hours. He's the spitting image of you. He's definitely got your nose, the same shape face as you. Oh, and your mouth. You look like him when you're sleeping.'

'His eyes might not be the same,' Sam pointed out.

'Well, you know all babies have blue eyes. They'll change—they'll turn the same beautiful silver-grey as his dad's,' she said confidently.

'Our baby boy.' Sam gently kissed the top of his son's head. 'Look, his hair's curly already. And he's fair, like you.'

'He's *perfect*,' she said proudly. And he was. Sam had done the paediatrician's check himself, no doubt haunted by what had happened to him as a baby, and he'd actually been in tears when he'd told Jodie everything was fine.

Her smile broadened. 'You know, Matt's going to be unbearably smug about the fact he shares our son's name, but I couldn't think of anything more appropriate. Matthew, gift of God. Our little boy.'

Sam met her gaze and smiled. 'We've been so lucky.'

'Haven't we just?'

Matthew Taylor gazed sleepily up at his father, moved his head to nuzzle Sam's chest, then realised that no milk was forthcoming. He opened his mouth and let out a loud howl of protest.

Sam chuckled. 'I'll change all the nappies you like, bath him and cuddle him and mop up any posseting— but this is definitely something he wants from his mum.' Gently, he handed the baby back to his wife, who leaned back against the pillow and adjusted Matthew's position until he could latch onto her breast. Sam watched them for a moment. 'You look like one of those Renaissance paintings,' he said, his lips curving. 'You know, Madonna and child.'

'They're supposed to be serene,' Jodie pointed out. 'Our son already knows his own mind—and he makes sure you know about it, too.'

'Just like his mum,' Sam teased, laughing.

'Huh. Aren't you supposed to be on ward rounds?'

'Uh-huh.'

'As in paediatric, not maternity?' she enunciated, amused.

'Detour,' he said simply. 'I was missing my wife—and my son.' He glanced at his watch and sighed. 'Actually, although I could stay here with you for ever, I'd better go. But I'll be back as soon as I've finished the ward rounds.' He leaned over to kiss her. 'I love you.'

'I love you, too.'

'And as for you, scrap, don't exhaust your mum too much.' He stroked the baby's cheek. 'I can't wait to take the pair of you home tomorrow. And show you off to everyone on the ward—Julianne's made a schedule of who's visiting and when.'

Jodie tried to keep a straight face but couldn't stop the giggles. 'A schedule?'

'To make sure you don't get overtired.' Sam's lips twitched.

'That's very sweet of her.' Jodie's smile broadened. 'But I don't give much for her chances. Most of them have already beaten her to it. Fi was the first one down, Mick babysat Charlie in the corridor while Shelley nipped in for a quick cuddle, then they swapped over, and Madge brought me a whole plate of lemon-curd tarts.'

'Where?' Sam demanded, looking round.

'Um, you've been beaten to them.'

'By half our ward?' he asked resignedly.

'Mmm. Duncan, Stuart, Megan and Sheila all had their fair share. Oh, and Lyn and Richard.' She smiled at him as Matthew decided he'd had enough milk and fell asleep again, clutching her finger tightly in one tiny fist. 'Life doesn't get any better than this, does it?'

'You wanted one of each,' he reminded her. 'We might need ICSI next time.'

'I'm happy right now,' Jodie said softly. 'Being here with the two men I love most in the world. A little girl, yes, that'd be the icing on the cake—to have one of each. But as long as I've got you, Sam, all's well with my world. And it always will be.'

He kissed her tenderly. 'Always,' he promised.

Modern Romance™
...seduction and
passion guaranteed

Tender Romance™
...love affairs that
last a lifetime

Sensual Romance™
...sassy, sexy and
seductive

Blaze.
...sultry days and
steamy nights

Medical Romance™
...medical drama on
the pulse

Historical Romance™
...rich, vivid and
passionate

27 new titles every month.

*With all kinds of Romance for
every kind of mood...*

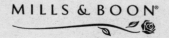

MILLS & BOON®

Medical Romance™

HOME BY CHRISTMAS by Jennifer Taylor

Christmas in the children's intensive care unit is always an emotional time, and especially so this year. Dr Lisa Bennett has until Christmas to decide whether to accept another man's proposal, and consultant surgeon Will Saunders has until Christmas Eve to help her realise that the life she should be daring to share — is his!

EMERGENCY: CHRISTMAS by Alison Roberts

Penny only started dating Dr Mark Wallace to make another man jealous — then discovered she'd done the right thing by accident! Their Christmas wedding would be perfect... But now the past was threatening to destroy their love — and a terrifying attack in the emergency room might mean they'd never get a second chance...

CHRISTMAS IN PARIS by Margaret Barker

When Dr Alyssa Ferguson returned to work in her beloved Paris, the last person she expected to see was her ex-lover, Pierre Dupont — and now he was her boss! As they began to rekindle their passionate romance, Pierre made Alyssa realise she had to face up to the past. Maybe they could look forward to a blissful Christmas in Paris together...

On sale 6th December 2002

1102/03b

CHRISTMAS
SECRETS

Three Festive Romances

CAROLE MORTIMER   CATHERINE SPENCER
DIANA HAMILTON

Available from 15th November 2002

Available at most branches of WH Smith,
Tesco, Martins, Borders, Eason, Sainsbury's
and all good paperback bookshops.

1202/59/MB50

FREE!

2 Books
and a surprise gift!

We would like to take this opportunity to thank you for reading this Mills & Boon® book by offering you the chance to take TWO more specially selected titles from the Medical Romance™ series absolutely FREE! We're also making this offer to introduce you to the benefits of the Reader Service™ —

★ FREE home delivery
★ FREE gifts and competitions
★ FREE monthly Newsletter
★ Books available before they're in the shops
★ Exclusive Reader Service discount

Accepting these FREE books and gift places you under no obligation to buy; you may cancel at any time, even after receiving your free shipment. Simply complete your details below and return the entire page to the address below. *You don't even need a stamp!*

YES! Please send me 2 free Medical Romance books and a surprise gift. I understand that unless you hear from me, I will receive 4 superb new titles every month for just £2.55 each, postage and packing free. I am under no obligation to purchase any books and may cancel my subscription at any time. The free books and gift will be mine to keep in any case.

M2ZEB

Ms/Mrs/Miss/Mr ....Initials................................
BLOCK CAPITALS PLEASE

Surname...

Address...

....

....Postcode ....

Send this whole page to:
UK: The Reader Service, FREEPOST CN81, Croydon, CR9 3WZ
EIRE: The Reader Service, PO Box 4546, Kilcock, County Kildare (stamp required)

Offer not valid to current Reader Service subscribers to this series. We reserve the right to refuse an application and applicants must be aged 18 years or over. Only one application per household. Terms and prices subject to change without notice. Offer expires 28th February 2003. As a result of this application, you may receive offers from Harlequin Mills & Boon and other carefully selected companies. If you would prefer not to share in this opportunity please write to The Data Manager at the address above.

Mills & Boon® is a registered trademark owned by Harlequin Mills & Boon Limited.
Medical Romance™ is being used as a trademark.